A Shade of Novak

A Shade of Vampire, Book 8

Bella Forrest

ALL RIGHTS RESERVED BY AUTHOR

Copyright © 2014 by Bella Forrest.
Cover design inspired by Sarah Hansen, Okay Creations LLC

This is a work of fiction.

All characters appearing in this book are fictitious. Any resemblance to real persons living or dead, other than those in the public domain, is not intended and purely coincidental.

No part of this book may be reproduced, re-sold, or transmitted electronically or otherwise, without express written permission from the author.

Also by Bella Forrest:

A SHADE OF VAMPIRE SERIES:
A Shade of Vampire (Book 1)
A Shade of Blood (Book 2)
A Castle of Sand (Book 3)
A Shadow of Light (Book 4)
A Blaze of Sun (Book 5)
A Gate of Night (Book 6)
A Break of Day (Book 7)
A Shade of Novak (Book 8)

A SHADE OF KIEV SERIES:
A Shade of Kiev 1
A Shade of Kiev 2

BEAUTIFUL MONSTER SERIES:
Beautiful Monster 1
Beautiful Monster 2

For an updated list of Bella's books, please visit www.bellaforrest.net

Contents

Prologue: Sofia 1
Chapter 1: Sofia 35
Chapter 2: Rose 47
Chapter 3: Derek 63
Chapter 4: Rose 67
Chapter 5: Rose 81
Chapter 6: Aiden 85
Chapter 7: Rose 95
Chapter 8: Sofia 101
Chapter 9: Rose 107
Chapter 10: Sofia 111
Chapter 11: Rose 115
Chapter 12: Sofia 119
Chapter 13: Rose 123
Chapter 14: Sofia 129
Chapter 15: Rose 133
Chapter 16: Rose 139
Chapter 17: Rose 147
Chapter 18: Rose 151
Chapter 19: Rose 155
Chapter 20: Rose 161

Chapter 21: Rose 167
Chapter 22: Rose 171
Chapter 23: Caleb 179
Chapter 24: Ben 183
Chapter 25: Rose 193
Chapter 26: Rose 199
Chapter 27: Rose 205
Chapter 28: Rose 211
Chapter 29: Caleb 215
Chapter 30: Rose 219
Chapter 31: Caleb 223
Chapter 32: Rose 239
Chapter 33: Rose 243
Chapter 34: Caleb 251
Chapter 35: Derek 255
Chapter 36: Rose 269
Chapter 37: Rose 277
Chapter 38: Caleb 283
Chapter 39: Rose 289
Chapter 40: Rose 293
Chapter 41: Aiden 297
Chapter 42: Sofia 301
Chapter 43: Caleb 303

Prologue: Sofia

"What did you just say?"

I didn't answer Derek for several moments as I continued staring at the television. Although the screen had changed, the image of two missing blonde twins remained etched in my mind.

Truth be told, I'd been considering this for some time now.

"You heard me," I said.

My husband sat bolt upright on the sofa next to me, his electric-blue eyes staring into mine. "But why?" He reached for my knee and gripped it.

"Because I'm worried, Derek."

He ran a hand through his thick dark hair, an exasperated expression on his face. "But how would this help?"

"After all we've been through… I just hate to feel powerless. Especially now that we have Ben and Rose."

"But after everything…" He trailed off, still staring at me disbelievingly. He glanced back at the television, which was showing photo after photo of missing people. Victims of kidnappings, the police assumed. Kidnappings that had become worse over the last couple of years.

We had been used to such things when the Elders and Hawks used to have a foothold on Earth. But they were banished now.

"We don't even know who is taking these people." Derek reached out to brush my cheek. "It could be humans at the bottom of this."

Even he seemed to lose conviction in his own words.

I raised a brow at him in disbelief.

"Eli and Ibrahim would disagree with you there," I said.

"Maybe." He sighed. "But they're not sure either."

"They're damn sure that whatever force is at work here isn't human. Something strange is going on. Derek, these people are just disappearing without a trace."

"But they still don't have any *evidence* that this is anything supernatural. This is all pure suspicion. And I'd say we're all biased to assume supernatural causes, wouldn't you agree?"

I sighed and leaned back against his chest. He wrapped his arms around me and kissed the top of my head.

"You're right," I said. "We don't have any evidence. But I still feel uneasy living here. We're smack-bam on one of the coastlines where these disappearances are going on."

We both fell silent. I snuggled closer against him, listening to the steady beat of his heart.

"You know what that would mean, right?" he asked finally.

I nodded and my throat went dry as all the implications washed over me. We both looked around the sitting room of our Californian dream home.

We'd have to sell this house and live in The Shade full time. Ben and Rose would have to leave all their friends. We'd say goodbye to making sandcastles on the beach together every Saturday afternoon. No more running around with them outside in the sunshine. Derek and I would once again become vampires.

I'd had this urge to turn back for a while. The main problem was that if I became a vampire again, Derek would have no choice but to do the same. Otherwise, I'd have to watch as Derek aged and passed away. He had fire-wielding capabilities and he still had superhuman strength thanks to Cora. But he didn't have immortality.

"I suppose it won't be that much of an upheaval for

them," Derek muttered. "They're still young. The Shade is already their second home during the summer holidays. And—"

I held a finger to Derek's lips. He was avoiding the subject.

"I know what this means for you," I whispered as he looked down at me. "I know how much you despised what you were before."

"I can't deny that the idea of being a vampire is associated with some pretty traumatic stuff in my past," he replied, smiling slightly at his understatement. "But you can't compare what it was like before to now. I'll have you to tame me." He kissed my cheek.

I looked wistfully again around the room. "And what will happen to this place?"

"Well, this is no longer your dream home if you're scared living in it." He shrugged. "And it's certainly no longer my dream home if you're unhappy here. We'll sell it."

I looked into his eyes again. Despite his trying to ease my guilt, I knew that turning back into a vampire would be a sacrifice. I couldn't have loved him more than at that moment for what he was willing to do to make me feel safe.

"Rose and Ben will have to get used to having vampires for parents," I muttered. "No more coming to us in the middle of the night for cozy time. We'll be the ones craving their warmth."

I thought again of our beautiful five-year-olds tucked up in bed upstairs. Rose with her long straight black hair, Ben with his shorter cut that stopped just above his ears, both sharing the same sparkling green eyes and long dark eyelashes. Derek was right that they were still too young for this to be too much of an upheaval. They made friends easily at this age. And they were used to The Shade. They had so many wellwishers back there—more than they even knew about. They were the sweethearts of the island, the little prince and princess. And everyone spoiled them rotten—especially Corrine.

Still, I couldn't shake the worry that I would be depriving them by sheltering them for the rest of their childhood on that small island. I would be depriving them of the more varied experiences they would have had if we'd stayed here and they'd attended a regular school, rather than the one run by the witches of The Shade. Although I had no doubt that those witches were far more knowledgeable and qualified than any junior-school teacher could be, I craved a life of normalcy for my children. Because normalcy was what I had always craved growing up. Normalcy was what I'd never had.

Derek stroked my head. "You're right for wanting this, darling. We're doing what's best for them. We're keeping them safe."

I nodded, although my throat still felt parched.

"We'll send them to summer camp once a year as soon as they're old enough," he continued. "Aiden can take them to Europe—far away from these kidnappings."

I nodded again. I couldn't deny that the idea of them going to summer camp made the weight on my chest a little lighter.

"I just want to shelter our children during these first few years," I said. "I want them to live without struggling or fearing. We owe them that much after the rough start they had in life."

Derek stood up, and, pulling me up toward him, placed both hands on the small of my back and drew me close to him. I wrapped my arms around his neck and held tight.

"One question that still remains is," he whispered, caressing my bare shoulder with his lips, "are we finished having children? Is two enough for us? Because… well, you know how it works."

I nodded. We would no longer be able to conceive once we were vampires.

Derek and I had discussed this before over the past five years. We'd gone back and forth on whether we wanted more children. But it always came down to the same fact: we both felt blessed with the children we had and hadn't felt the urge to have more. They were five years old now, and we still hadn't made plans for more.

Still, it was a heavy question to answer, knowing that now it would be final. Unless of course we were both willing to take the cure again and turn back into humans.

We both stood in each other's arms in silence for what felt like an eternity. Finally we looked into each other's eyes.

"I think we are," I said quietly.

He nodded in agreement.

Then an obvious question struck me. "But do we even know you can be turned?"

"We'll have to consult with Ibrahim and get his opinion."

"Because if there's a risk, then—"

"There's no point speculating," Derek said, holding up a hand. "We'll ask him what the risks are."

I nodded and gulped down the lump in my throat.

"Derek," I said, removing my arms from round his neck and clutching his hands in mine. "If you can be turned and we go through with this, we must promise not to tell our children why we left the outside world and moved to The Shade. I don't want them growing up in fear."

"I don't like the idea of them growing up naive," Derek said, looking down at me seriously. "Oblivious to the world around them. That's dangerous."

"I know," I said, sighing. "I know we can't hide them away from the world forever. But I want to wait at least until they're older, in their late teens."

Derek paused and continued looking at me. Eventually he nodded.

"Seventeen," he said. "We'll wait until they're seventeen. Agreed?"

"Agreed."

We continued staring at each other, the gravity of what we were planning to do settling upon us.

"Have you considered that, unless Rose and Ben turn too, they could end up older than us?" Derek said.

"Oh. That would be... strange," I said slowly, trying to wrap my head around the notion. "Really... really strange."

"They would have to turn before they reached our age," he said, running a hand through my hair. "But what if they're immunes, like you used to be?"

"That's unlikely. According to the witches, immunity to vampirism normally skips a generation. But still, it's something we'll have to discuss with them when they're older," I said. "There's no point thinking about it now. So much could happen between now and then. We still have a good few years ahead of us before that time comes."

"Hm." A grin spread across Derek's face, mischief sparking in his eyes. "So you'll be my forever sexy twenty-three-year-old wife."

I smirked.

"And you my forever sexy twenty-four-year-old husband… well, technically you're also twenty-three, actually—"

"Enough with pedantries."

Before I could object, he swept me off my feet and carried me up the stairs to our bedroom. Laying me down on our bed, he began slipping off my nightdress. He paused, the smile on his face fading.

"If we're really planning to go through with this, it ought to be sooner rather than later. Because…" He trailed off and looked down at me seriously, so much that I held my breath, wondering what was wrong. He leant down, as though examining me. "I can already see a wrinkle forming in the corner of your eye."

I giggled and slapped him on the shoulder.

"Derek! We shouldn't be making light of this situation. We still have a lot to—"

"Yes, we still have a lot to do," he whispered, his voice husky, "While we're both still warm."

He finished pulling off my nightdress and then ripped off his own clothes. My skin tingled as his heated body slid beneath the sheets next to me.

Sometimes when we made love, in Derek's abandon, he would become almost too fiery for me to touch and we had to stop until he calmed down a little. On a few occasions, the sheets he had been gripping had become singed.

No, a change of temperature wouldn't necessarily be a bad thing for my husband.

*****

Over the next month, we arranged the sale of the house—which thankfully wasn't difficult due to its location—and made final arrangements for leaving. We packed up all of our belongings and made sure that Ben and Rose had an opportunity to bid farewell to all their pre-school friends.

When asked by our neighbors and other parents where we were going, we told them that we had decided to relocate to Europe to be close to an ailing relative.

My father, Aiden, arrived on the doorstep the night before the new owners were due to take possession of the house. He was dressed casually in a loose short-sleeved shirt and jeans. I'd told the twins to sit by the door on some suitcases so that they were out of the way, but they jumped up as soon as their grandfather walked through the door.

"It's Grandpa!" Rose squealed.

"Grandpa!" Ben yelled.

Aiden's face lit up as soon as he saw them. He had gotten rid of his Hawk form thanks to Ibrahim who, after several years experimenting with a combination of spells and potions, had finally managed to transform him back into a human with the help of several other witches.

My father wrapped his arms around each of them, planting kisses on their foreheads. I walked over to him and kissed his cheek.

"Thanks for being on time," I said. I turned around and called, "Derek, Grandpa's here."

Derek walked out of the kitchen with our final suitcase. He put the case down on the floor and smiled at Aiden, "Hello, Grandpa."

"Hello," Aiden said, smiling back. "Xavier and Vivienne are waiting in the sub in the usual place."

It had been four months since we'd last visited The Shade. Excitement bubbled up inside me at the prospect of seeing my sister and brother-in-law again.

Aiden headed straight to the submarine to drop off Ben and Rose. Then he returned to help Derek and I carry the rest of our luggage down to the harbor. It took us several shifts until we had it all moved. We'd included all our furniture in the sale of the house, but it was amazing how many personal belongings we had accumulated after having children.

Once we'd finished, we knocked on the hatch and Vivienne pushed it open. She looked radiant as she smiled down at me, happiness showing in her laughter lines, her violet-blue eyes sparkling.

Derek, Aiden and I lowered ourselves inside and fastened the hatch above us.

"I've missed you so much!" Vivienne gushed.

She pulled Derek and I into an embrace and kissed our cheeks. She led us into the control room at the front of the submarine and we each took a seat.

I smiled on seeing Ben and Rose already there sitting on Uncle Xavier's lap. They loved the control room. Their eyes were filled with wonder as they fiddled around with different buttons and muttered to each other.

"Welcome to my abode." Xavier grinned.

Derek gripped Xavier's shoulder and ruffled his hair, while I placed a kiss on his cheek. Then Derek turned to his sister and, pointing at Xavier, asked, "Has this scoundrel been treating you right since I've been away?"

Vivienne grinned and placed a hand on Xavier's shoulder. "Oh, yes. He has."

"Good."

Vivienne turned to the twins, "Hey, Rose. Ben. Aren't you going to give Aunty a hug?"

They pried their eyes away from the controls. Toothy smiles spread across their faces as they looked up at Vivienne. They reached out their arms so she could pick them both up. She showered their faces with kisses and carried them out of the control room toward the back of the submarine.

"We're all… uh… intrigued, to say the least, to hear that you've decided to become creatures of the night once again," Xavier said, as he began to navigate the vessel away from the harbor.

I looked at my father. I'd discussed our plans with him already over the phone, and he'd seemed to understand my reasons for wanting to turn back. Apparently sensing my uncertainty about his true feelings, he reached out and gripped my knee, smiling.

"I think we were all surprised," Aiden said. "But I'm sure everyone in The Shade will be glad to have their queen and king return to their full-time duties."

Vivienne entered without the twins. When I looked up, she pointed toward the back of the sub where Rose and Ben sat on a bench munching their way through a bowl of strawberries.

"Corrine insisted on sending a snack for them for the journey," she said, smiling.

Vivienne took a seat in the front row next to Xavier and we spent the rest of the trip answering questions about our decision.

Finally, Xavier raised a brow and looked at me and Derek.

"So… assuming Ibrahim says that it's safe to try turning Derek back into a bloodsucker, have you decided who will turn you both?"

Derek and I exchanged glances.

"That should be obvious," Derek said, looking back at Xavier and raising an eyebrow. "You shall have the great privilege of turning me, while Vivienne will turn Sofia."

"Oh…" Xavier said, a look of mock disappointment crossing his face. "I think I'd have more fun turning Sofia. I'm not overly keen on the idea of biting into your thick neck."

Vivienne elbowed Xavier in the gut and said, "No, Sofia's mine. All mine."

I giggled and, looking at Derek, shrugged.

"Seems nobody wants poor Mr. Derek. Maybe I'll have to turn you myself."

I'd meant it as a joke, but his eyes lit up. "Yes, Sofia. Why not? Why don't you turn me? I'd much rather have you sucking at my neck than this ugly bloke," he said, shoving Xavier in the shoulder.

I looked at Derek nervously.

"Are you serious?"

"Yes. I'm serious," he said, staring back. "Vivienne will turn you, and then you'll turn me."

My stomach writhed.

"Why doesn't Vivienne just turn you after me?"

He looked at Vivienne, then back to me. "I just think that it would be more interesting if you turned me." He raised a brow at me, a small smile curling his lips.

"Actually, what if you can't be turned? You need to go first, because if you don't turn, then I can't turn."

"Well, let's see what Ibrahim says," he replied. "If he says I can be turned, then we'll take his word for it."

"But, Derek," I spluttered. "I've never turned anybody before. What if I do something wrong?"

He stared at me for a moment, considering the possibility.

"Well, Xavier and Vivienne will be there to guide you… and haul you off of me if necessary."

*****

Barely had the hatch of the submarine opened when cheers erupted. I picked up Rose, while Derek carried Ben, and we all climbed out of the submarine.

A small crowd was standing by the port to welcome us. Tears welled in my eyes as I looked around at the familiar faces.

I had to quickly hand Rose over to my father as Shadow was the first to reach us. His tongue wagging, he jumped up at me to lick me, almost knocking me over in the process. He had broken free from Eli, who now came hurrying over with a wide grin on his face.

"I hear you've decided to come back over to the dark side again, Sofia." Claudia smirked and winked at me.

"Welcome."

Zinnia bared her fangs at me and chuckled. Gavin gave me a friendly punch on the shoulder. "Good to have you back, girl."

"Rose!"

Griffin, their four-year-old son, stepped out from behind Gavin. His curly red hair reminded me so much of his father, while his hazelnut brown eyes were decidedly his mother's. He made a dash for Rose and wrapped his arms around her, placing a kiss on her cheek. I smiled as Rose blushed.

"Hello Griffin," she mumbled.

Griffin had been a surprise for Zinnia and Gavin. He'd been conceived while they were travelling and helping Aiden disband the worldwide organization of hunters. Only recently had the couple decided to turn into vampires, once they'd deemed their little human boy old enough to handle the shock of mom and dad sprouting fangs.

It saddened me to think of two vampires who would not be waiting to greet us: Liana and Cameron. Even though it had been years, we still missed their company. They had taken the cure to become humans and left the island. Their children and grandchildren had passed away, but they'd had a burning desire to search out any family living today. They'd told us they would likely return to The Shade after a few years, but we were still waiting for them.

Once we'd finished greeting everyone who'd been waiting at the Port, Derek and I took the twins' hands and led them toward the forest. But as we were about to enter the woods, something stirred in the trees. A small vampire walked out. Abby.

She looked at me and smiled faintly. Something about her was off.

"Abby!" I said.

She came to us and I put my arms around her, hugging her close. I pulled her away so I could examine her face more closely.

"What's wrong?" I asked quietly.

A tear rolled down Abby's cheek and her lip trembled.

"I want to turn back into a human, Sofia," she said. "I want to grow up."

I breathed in deeply. I felt the pain in her voice. I'd actually been expecting this day to come sooner. She should be reaching her adolescent years by now, yet she was still trapped in the body of a child.

"We'll do it, Abby. I promise. We'll turn you back into a human before this month is over."

I placed a kiss on her head and she smiled more fully, reassured by my promise. She kissed my cheek and drew away from me, allowing me to continue forward with Derek, Vivienne, Xavier and the twins.

"Sofia! Derek!"

I turned around yet again. Anna walked toward us, her long black hair flowing down her back as she carried her and Kyle's one-year-old daughter, Ariana, in her arms. Kyle followed closely behind her. I kissed them all and while Anna stayed to talk with me, Kyle walked over to Derek, who started talking animatedly with him.

Ariana reminded me of Rose when she was younger. She was a beautiful child and had similar features—green eyes and dark hair.

"Anna!" Ben shouted. He left Derek's side and wandered over to us.

Anna beamed and bent down to cuddle him. It warmed my heart to see the special bond the two of them had, and I felt an eternal sense of gratitude. If it wasn't for Anna's initiative to take care of Ben when he was still a newborn trapped in Aviary, I doubted I ever would have seen him again.

Rose also skipped over and tugged on Anna's sleeve.

"Hey Anna and Ariana," she said, smiling sweetly.

"Hey beautiful." Anna kissed Rose's cheeks.

"Sofia," Anna said, after she'd finished greeting the twins. "Ian left."

I stared at her. "Already?"

She nodded. "He finally proposed to Katrine about a

month ago, and they decided it was time to leave the island and start their new life outside. He was sorry you weren't here to say goodbye."

I smiled. Ian and Katrine—one of the human girls who used to live a few doors along from him in the Catacombs—had started seeing each other three years ago.

While I was deeply disappointed that he hadn't waited to say goodbye to us, I felt nothing but happiness for them. I saw joy in Anna's eyes too, and an obvious relief. Ian had finally found someone to replace her, and he no longer had to suffer each time he saw her with Kyle.

"Well, I'll let you go, Sofia," Anna said. "I'm sure you've got lots of work to do settling into your home again. I'll see you around."

She kissed me once more and headed off with Kyle and Ariana.

Derek scooped up Ben and placed him on his shoulders. Ben chuckled with delight on being so high up. I took Rose's hand and kissed her on the nose, which made her giggle.

As we neared the Residences, two more familiar faces came into view. Ashley and Landis—Xavier's younger brother—were walking toward us, holding hands.

It had taken Ashley two years to finally let Landis in after she had lost Sam in the most brutal way imaginable. But finally, the day had come when she was happy again.

I ran up to Ashley, pulling her into my arms. I kissed her cold pale cheek and whispered, "I missed you so much."

Tears welled in my eyes as she smiled back at me. I'd grown so used to her smiling only to stop people pitying her. But now she was smiling from her heart. She'd truly found happiness with Landis.

I stayed with Ashley for several more minutes before finally turning away and arriving at the foot of one of the tallest redwood trees on the island, upon which our magnificent penthouse was built. We stepped into the glass elevator and made our way to the top.

Rose and Ben wandered about on the verandah, marveling at the star-strewn sky. We'd made sure to build a high fence around the verandah so that there was no chance of any accidents. Our twins had dangerously adventurous minds and, now that they were becoming independent, it was hard to keep an eye on them sometimes.

Once we'd settled down and finished bringing our luggage up, we left the twins in their playroom with Aiden watching over them and left the house with Vivienne and Xavier.

We headed back through the woods until we reached the clearing outside the witches' temple. Corrine's Sanctuary. We knocked on the wooden double doors and Corrine opened them a few moments later.

"Well, hello," she said, grinning. "Come in."

We followed her along narrow corridors until we reached a circular study lined with shelves of bottled potions.

Ibrahim looked up from his seat at a small table in the corner of the room.

"Welcome back!" He stood up and gave us both a hug.

We took seats around the table, while Corrine sat herself down on Ibrahim's lap.

"So," Corrine began, raising an eyebrow and eyeing us closely. "You both really want to turn back again."

Derek and I exchanged glances before nodding.

"But we need to know what the situation with Derek is," I said. "Do you think he can be turned back—with his fire powers and all?"

Ibrahim stroked his chin and continued staring at us, deep in thought.

"Well," he said, "we still don't know exactly what kind of spell Cora cast on you to give you those powers. But I am quite certain that it won't interfere with you turning back. You were a vampire before. I don't see why you can't be one again."

I looked at Derek, gripping his hand.

"Well, let's do this," he said.

*****

After we returned to our penthouse, we finished unpacking and then spent the rest of the evening with Ben and Rose. This would be the last night we'd spend with them as humans. Derek and I had decided that Vivienne would turn me the next day. Assuming I felt steady enough after the transformation, the plan was for me to turn Derek the same day.

The twins slept cuddled up with us that night in our warm bed. We slept in late the next morning and had breakfast in bed. I cooked up their favorite: hash browns with cheese and tomato sauce.

Aiden arrived at about eleven o'clock in the morning and kept the twins occupied in their playroom while we left. He'd promised to look after them until we were in a fit state to see them again.

Derek and I held hands as we neared the clearing by the Port. Vivienne had suggested that we do the turning here since there was lots of open space and nothing easily destructible for almost a mile radius around us.

As we neared, my unease grew. Knots formed in my stomach. A small crowd had gathered around the clearing, all familiar faces. I gulped as I looked at Vivienne waiting in the center of the clearing, where a wide stone slab had been placed. She smiled at me as I approached her and gave my hand a reassuring squeeze.

"I'll be gentle with you," she said.

As gentle as a vampire can be while ripping into a human's throat.

I remembered the time I'd witnessed Ashley's turning in the Sanctuary. Kyle had done it. Ashley had writhed around in agony for what felt like hours. There'd been nothing anyone could do to help ease the pain. She had described it afterwards as being a torture so unbearable that you began willing yourself to die.

But I wondered if it was anything near the agony of turning from vampire to human. I shivered, recalling the sensation of the sun roasting me alive. I had done that and survived.

This can't be worse than that. Nothing *can be worse than that.*

The crowd was deathly silent as I positioned myself flat on the stone. Derek bent over me and placed a tender kiss on my lips.

"I'm right here with you," he said. "I'll be by your side the whole time."

I gulped and nodded.

My heart began to race as Derek stepped back and Vivienne leant down so that her face was level with mine.

As she brushed the hair away from my neck and bared her fangs, I looked up at Derek once more and locked eyes with him.

That was when it hit me what was truly bothering me about this whole situation.

"Wait!" I gasped, pushing Vivienne away just before she broke skin.

"What?" She frowned at me.

I sat up and rushed over to Derek, taking him by the hand. "I need to have a quick word with Derek first, okay? We'll be right back."

Derek looked just as bewildered as Vivienne as I dragged him back into the woods. I walked with him until we were out of view of the others, then stared up at him.

"I want you to turn me, Derek."

His eyes widened.

"Huh? Why? We already agreed that you would turn me."

Oh, God. How do I say this?

I paused and felt my cheeks blush crimson. I had to avert my eyes to the ground as I stuttered, "It's a... fantasy I have. You turning me. Ever since the beginning."

It was a fantasy that I'd kept hidden deep within my subconscious ever since I'd first met him. I'd always imagined that if I ever turned, he would be the one to do it. I'd never even admitted this to myself until now.

The words sounded so awkward that my face burned with embarrassment.

He reached beneath my chin and pushed it up so I was forced to face him. His intense eyes bored into me.

"What if I have a fantasy about you turning me?" he asked softly.

I couldn't help but giggle at the seriousness of Derek's questioning glare.

"Then you'll be a gentleman and grant your lady her fantasy."

He frowned at me for a moment, studying me closely. Then he nodded in defeat. "Hm."

He wrapped an arm around my waist and led me back into the clearing.

"Change of plan, everybody," he announced. "I've decided that I want to turn Sofia. So Vivienne will turn me first."

Vivienne looked surprised, as did everybody else. But Derek didn't leave time for questions. He walked straight over to the slab and lay down.

Vivienne looked down at him, frowning. Then she sighed and lowered herself down to her brother's level.

My heart raced as Vivienne bared her fangs and in one sharp movement dug them into Derek's neck. I rushed over to the other side of the stone, where I could get a clearer view of Derek. But Xavier gripped my arm and pulled me back.

"We don't know what state he'll be in once he's turned.

Best you keep your distance."

I stepped back to stand with everyone else. Ashley reached for my hand and squeezed it.

"Stop worrying," she whispered. "Derek's a warrior. He'll get through this."

Her words did little to ease my nerves as Derek began to shake violently.

Vivienne would never harm her brother, but I couldn't stop my heart palpitations as Derek's convulsions worsened. By the time Vivienne drew away from him, wiping his blood away from her lips, he was shaking so violently that Xavier and Yuri had to grip his arms to hold him down against the slab.

And then the blood came. Derek began heaving up mouthfuls of it. Ashley's hold around me tightened as I once again tried to run forward.

"The blood is a good sign, Sofia," she whispered. "It means that Vivienne's venom is working."

I tried to breathe more calmly.

It's a good sign. It's a good sign. I repeated the words in my head like a prayer.

Finally, Derek stopped coughing and his body flattened on the stone. Though his hands and feet still twitched, Xavier and Yuri let go of him and stepped away. Ashley's hold on me also loosened as I relaxed.

His eyes remained shut tight. His body now seemed too still for comfort. Before when he was shaking, at least he was giving obvious signs that he was alive. But now that he lay so deathly still…

Before Ashley could stop me, I broke away from the crowd and ran toward the slab.

Xavier and Yuri whirled around.

"No!" they shouted. "Don't come so close. Your blood—"

Ashley grabbed me by my midriff and dragged me backward.

"Stop it, Sofia!" she hissed against my ear. "Xavier already told you we don't know what state he's going to be in when he wakes up."

But it was too late.

Derek's eyes shot open and he sat bolt upright, wiping away the blood from his face with his sleeve.

He turned his head toward my direction and his blazing eyes—now several shades brighter—settled on me.

The lion had smelt its prey.

Xavier and Yuri hurled themselves at him, but he threw them out of his way with force I'd forgotten Derek ever possessed.

Ashley and Claudia jumped forward to shield me from him, but he brushed them aside too. Grabbing hold of my waist, he flung me over his shoulder and raced into the woods.

"No!" I screamed. "Derek, stop!"

He continued moving forward with frightening speed. Only once I could no longer hear the others chasing after us did he stop beneath the foot of a tree. He lowered me to the ground and, gripping my neck between his strong hands, pushed me back against the tree. Then he placed one hand over my mouth to stifle my scream, using the other to brush the hair away from my neck, giving him clear access. His eyes gleamed with a hunger that made me believe he could suck me dry within minutes.

Oh, no. Not again.

This isn't happening.

This can't be happening.

I'd thought that he'd be the same vampire he was just before he turned into a human. I hadn't thought he'd revert to the uncontrollable bloodsucker he'd been when he'd first woken up after his four-hundred-year sleep. It hadn't even occurred to me. But now, to my horror, everything about this situation reminded me of that time. The way he had rammed me up against a hard surface, his eyes burning, his cool breath against my skin.

Everything felt identical to the day we'd first met.

What about our children?

I did the only thing I could think to do in the past

whenever Derek lost control of himself. I began humming our tune. Even though his hand was placed over my mouth, I hummed it as loudly as possible.

"Silence." His voice came as a growl. "Your little tune won't work any more."

What?

His chest heaving and eyes ablaze, he lowered his head to my throat. I gasped as his fangs scraped against my neck, his cold tongue running along my skin.

I was beginning to lose all hope that I'd be able to get through to him in time when his grip loosened. I felt him step away.

When I opened my eyes, gone was the look of mad bloodlust.

In its place was Derek's boyish grin.

As soon as my eyes met his, he doubled over and began laughing.

"You should have seen the look on your face!" he gasped.

My mouth fell open. The blood rushed back to my cheeks.

"Oh my God, Derek!" I breathed.

"You looked so adorable… and when you tried to hum our tune." He caught my face between his hands and pressed his lips against mine. "I'm sorry. It was all too easy. I just couldn't resist."

"You almost gave me a heart attack."

He broke out laughing again, and this time I couldn't stop myself from joining in, even though I was still quivering in my shoes from the shock.

"I thought we were all the way back to square one," I said. "All that work I put into you, all for nothing."

"No," he said, his chest still heaving as he tried to contain his laughter. "I suppose whatever progress I made when I was a vampire before, I've retained… luckily for you."

He raised a brow at me and pulled me against him, breathing into my neck.

"That said, you do smell rather tempting."

"Well, you can have a bite of me later," I muttered, looking up as the others came racing toward us.

They stared at us, their faces white with panic. The terror in their eyes turned to confusion as they watched us both acting as if nothing had happened.

"All of that," I said, glaring at Derek, "was your king's idea of a joke."

*****

"So what does it feel like to be a vampire again?" I asked.

We were in Vivienne's penthouse, in one of her spare rooms. Derek lay on his back on the bed while I rested beside him, holding his hand in mine.

"It's… strange. Now that I've spent time away from it, I don't detest it as much as I used to. I suppose it's also a relief to not be constantly worrying about fire bursting from my palms whenever I get too, uh, excited."

He winked at me. I grinned back at him.

I'd suggested that he rest after the trauma of the morning, in order to prepare for what he was to do. Now it was nighttime.

We both fell silent. Now that the time we had agreed upon had approached, blood rushed to my cheeks again. I was sure that we were both thinking the same thing.

I bit my lip as I looked up at him. His face was now serious, his eyes intense.

"Well," I muttered. "I guess it's time."

Without another word, he stood up and, scooping me up in his arms, walked out of the room. As we passed the living room, we saw Vivienne and Xavier sitting together on the couch.

"You're going to do it now?" she asked.

Derek nodded.

They both got up and approach us, but Derek shook his head.

"We won't be needing either of you. I can handle her… whatever state she might be in once she's turned."

He rushed out before either of them could respond. We

took the elevator down to the ground and he began whipping through the trees. His speed left me struggling to breathe as I tightened my hold around him.

We passed right by the clearing where Vivienne had turned Derek earlier.

"Where are we going?"

"You do realize that this is the last night we'll both be the way we were when we first met? When I first fell in love with you."

I nodded as his words sank in.

Derek, a vampire. Me, a human.

We ran along the beach, along the outskirts of the wall, until we reached a cluster of giant boulders. He climbed up over them. After a few minutes, it came into view.

The lighthouse.

All the memories that came with the place washed over me and I had to fight to hold back tears.

He approached it and sped up the stairs. Once we reached the top, he pushed the door open to the cozy circular room and laid me down on the four-poster bed we had brought up here especially for occasions when we took time away from everybody.

He walked around the room, drawing the red velvet curtains and lighting the candles that surrounded the bed.

"I had my fun earlier," he said, approaching the bed and

looking down at me through his dark lashes. "Now this is your night, Sofia. Your fantasy."

My throat went dry as he removed his shirt, revealing his ripped torso.

"So, baby. What would you like to do first?"

"I… I, uh…"

He cocked his head to one side.

"Sofia Novak tongue-tied? What's wrong?" He ripped off his jeans in one sudden movement, revealing his underwear. "Do I intimidate you?"

I swallowed hard.

He knelt down on the bed and pushed me back. Crawling over me until his face was above mine, he held my arms over my head.

What is wrong with me? I was breathless as a teenager whose first crush had just walked into the room.

I closed my eyes as his lips found the softest, most sensitive part of my neck, just beneath my ear. He ran his tongue against it, then I sensed the slightest scrape of his fangs.

I exhaled sharply.

"Do you want this, Sofia?" he whispered, reaching behind my back and unzipping my dress.

"Yes," I breathed.

"Do you really want it?" he asked, pulling the dress over

my head and unclasping my bra.

"Yes."

Gripping the front of my bra between his teeth, he tossed it over his shoulder. Then he lowered his head to my panties and, biting through the elastic, disposed of them too.

"And you want me to do it to you?" he asked, now running his wide palms along my thighs.

"Duh," I gasped.

The shadow of a smile crossed his lips.

I shivered as he positioned himself over my hips.

"All right," he whispered. "If you insist."

Chapter 1: Sofia

Twelve years later...

"Summer camp at seventeen. Are you serious, Mom?"

I stared at my daughter. Her long dark hair was tied up in a ponytail, her beautiful green eyes fixed on me.

My Rose. Princess of The Shade.

"Ben!" she called.

The door swung open and her brother came storming into the dining room.

"You're not going to believe this," she said, rolling her eyes in my direction. "Mom wants us to go to summer camp *again* this year."

"What?"

Ben, my prince. He looked so much like his father it was uncanny. He towered above us, looking from me to Rose. As soon as he laid eyes on his sister, his expression mimicked hers. He turned on me.

"Seriously, Mom? Last year, okay, but this year? We're way too old."

I couldn't help but giggle at their outrage. "Oh, I'm sorry, old man," I said, patting his shoulder. "Are your knees playing up again?"

"Dad!" Ben called. When Derek didn't answer, Ben went storming back out of the room in search of him.

"Hey, Mom. Can I have an early birthday present?" Rose asked, looking up at me innocently through her long dark lashes.

"What?"

"Don't send me to summer camp," she deadpanned.

"You two!" I said. "It's not the same one you went to last time. It's not even called a summer camp. It's a survival training course. It'll be heaps of fun. It's on a little island off the coast of Scotland. Look, here's the brochure. As you can see on the first page, this is for ages seventeen to twenty-five, so you'll be the youngest ones there. Granddad's already booked it and—"

"Oh, so it's old enough for both of my parents to go.

That's great," Rose said, eyeing the brochure. "How about you two go instead of us?"

"Watch it," Derek said, as he entered the room with Ben. He was still dressed in his pajamas and was carrying a book under his arm. "The two of you aren't going to make it to seventeen if you're not careful." Derek bared his fangs at Rose. "You'll forever be almost-seventeen-year-old vampires." He caught hold of Ben and nuzzled him.

Ben ducked out of Derek's grip and walked over to his sister, standing at the opposite side of the table from us. "Did you agree to this?" Ben stared at his father accusingly.

"Oh, yes," Derek said. "In fact, I was the one who suggested it."

They both groaned.

"Why do you want us to go so much?" Rose asked.

"We've been through this before, sweetheart." I sighed. "This is going to be your last year of having the opportunity to go outside and be normal. You keep saying you want to turn into vampires. Well, this is the price we're making you pay, because you'll thank us for it five hundred years from now. You'll think back on this time fondly."

"Five hundred years stuck with you two," Ben muttered under his breath. "Maybe I'll stay a human."

"You've been begging us to turn you since you were eight years old," I reminded him.

He fell silent.

"Now," I said. "You're leaving the day after your birthday. That's in three days' time. So I suggest you start packing now. Look at this list of stuff to take and let me know if there's anything we don't have."

With that, I caught Derek's hand and we left the room.

"They complain every year," I said to him. "But when they come back they've had the time of their lives. Teenagers. They have to find something to complain about or their day isn't complete." I kissed Derek's cheek and said, "I'm going to see Corrine."

"All right, baby," he said, retreating into his study.

I left the penthouse and made my way toward the Sanctuary. I knocked on the door. Ibrahim answered, holding a mug of some type of exotic-smelling spiced tea in his hand.

"Hi, Ibrahim."

"Hello, Sofia. How can I help?"

"I'm here for Corrine. Is she in?"

"No, she's at the school."

I thanked him and walked back through the woods until I reached The Shade's bustling town center—the Vale. The school was in a large white building in the middle of the main square. I entered and walked through the corridors, scanning each classroom as I went. I stopped suddenly as I caught sight of my father—now a vampire—leaning against a desk in one of the classrooms. He was talking to Adelle, the headmistress of the school. She was a tall, striking auburn-haired witch who looked as though she was in her mid-thirties.

She'd arrived on the island seventeen years ago, along with Ibrahim and a group of other witches who'd abandoned The Sanctuary in favor of living with us. We were indebted to these witches in so many ways. We could not have rebuilt The Shade into what it was today without them. Before they arrived, thanks to The Elders and their children, our island had been a complete wreck. Now, the island was better and more beautiful than ever before.

"Oh, hi, Sofia," Aiden said, noticing me by the door.

It was still bizarre to see him as a vampire. He had finally caved in about a year after Derek and I had become vampires. He'd detested himself at first, but over the years he'd grown used to it. Recently I'd noticed him having some particularly long conversations with Adelle. I hadn't dared ask him about their friendship yet, but I couldn't miss the attraction that sparked in his eyes every time he laid eyes on her. It warmed my heart that he might finally be opening up to another woman. And this time, to a woman who deserved him.

"Hi, Dad," I said. "Don't mind me."

I smiled to myself as I left them in privacy. I continued walking along the corridors in hopes of spotting Corrine. That was when I saw Abby. She was sitting behind a desk in a small office, shuffling papers and making notes.

She looked up as soon as I entered. Abigail Hudson was now a beautiful young woman, her long blonde hair wrapped in a neat bun above her head, her light blue eyes gazing at me. Her resemblance to her brother was so striking I often found myself needing to take a few moments aside after speaking to her, as tears threatened to spill down my cheeks.

Years ago, we'd turned her back into a human so she could grow up. She'd remained as one until she reached eighteen, and then she'd wanted to turn back into a vampire. I'd turned her myself. Now she worked here alongside the witches as a school teacher, and she clearly adored every moment of it.

"Hi, Sofia," she said, grinning. "How can I help?"

"Do you know where Corrine is?" I asked. "Ibrahim said she was here in the school somewhere."

"She's with Anna in the dining hall."

"Thanks, Abby."

I turned and left the room. Arriving in the dining hall—a large high-ceilinged room with long wooden tables running the length of it—I saw Corrine sitting with Anna in the far corner.

They appeared deep in conversation, so I waited by the door, but my acute sense of hearing couldn't help but pick up on their conversation.

"I think we'll only need one more round of blood," Corrine said. "After that, I'm sure we have enough to recreate more samples from what you've given us over the years. We've stored it all carefully."

Of course. Corrine had mentioned to me that she'd be having this conversation with Anna. Since Anna was now the only immune that we had on this island, her blood was immensely valuable.

She'd given us generous amounts of her blood so that we could store it and use it for any vampires who wanted to turn back into humans. Over the years, the witches had managed to develop a way to duplicate her blood and mix it with animal blood that would have the same effect when consumed by a vampire. Had they not done this, too much of Anna's blood would have been needed to ensure that we would never run out. The witches stored the samples securely in three separate parts of the island—that way even if disaster happened, it was unlikely that we'd lose everything. Vampires would continue to have the option to turn back into humans, even after Anna died.

Anna's straight black hair flowed down her shoulders, her eyes on Corrine. When she wasn't giving blood or spending time with her family, she assisted in the island's pre-school. She was well into her thirties now, and a large bump protruded from her stomach. This would be her third child with Kyle.

It was strange to think that I would be her age now had I not asked Derek to turn me. My heart ached as I looked at her. I owed her more than I could ever repay. Yet I felt powerless to hold on to her.

Since Anna was immune to the vampire curse, there was no way she could ever become one of us. Immortal. The only way we knew to cure an immune of their immunity was to take them to Cruor—as I had been kidnapped there. That was a fate worse than death, and it wasn't even possible, since the gates to that realm had been closed for almost two decades.

We all had to accept the fact that she would pass away. It was for that reason that Kyle hadn't changed himself back into a vampire. He couldn't stand the idea of living on without her, so he'd decided that he would pass away naturally with her when nature took them both.

"It's not a problem, Corrine." Anna smiled gently. "I've always told you that I don't mind giving blood. I'm glad that it's so useful."

"Yes." Corrine squeezed her hand. "And this island owes you too much already, Anna. We don't want to take anything more from you than we absolutely need."

"It's fine, Corrine," Anna said, waving a hand in the air. "You're all my family."

Corrine sighed and stood up. "Well, I won't keep you any longer, dear," she said, eyeing Anna's huge stomach. "You take it easy, all right?"

Anna nodded and walked over to the exit at the other side of the room, while Corrine made her way toward me. "Ah, Sofia. I've been expecting you." She looped an arm through mine and we left the dining hall. "Let's go back to my place."

"So you definitely won't need to take any more of Anna's blood after this?" I asked.

"That's correct. We have enough to recreate more doses, so long as we guard our supply carefully."

I sighed heavily.

Corrine looked up at me. "Anna's at peace with her life," she said. "You fret more about her than she does for herself. You do realize that?"

I nodded. "I just can't stand the thought of losing her one day. It will be like losing a sister."

"I know," Corrine replied, clenching her jaw. "There's not a person on this island who won't grieve her loss. That one's special. Kyle's a very lucky man."

We walked in silence for the rest of the walk to the Sanctuary. Once we were sitting in Corrine's lounge, I tried to tear my mind away from Anna. From her fate that I had no power over.

"So," I said, clearing my throat. "About the twins' birthday…"

Corrine's eyes lit up with excitement as she began explaining to me the ideas she had for their party this year.

I held up a hand.

"Corrine, this is what I'm here to talk to you about. They don't want us to throw them a big party this year."

Her face fell in disappointment.

"Why ever not? We always have so much fun."

"They're… maturing. They don't like the idea of their parents still organizing parties for them. I'm already making them go on that adventure course. They won't want a big party as well. We can just arrange for a picnic for all the children and teenagers on this island."

Corrine swallowed back her disappointment and nodded.

"Well… all right then."

I squeezed her shoulder. The witch—still holding out on having children of her own with Ibrahim, since, being a witch, she still had lots of youthful years ahead of her—lavished all her attention on the twins and enjoyed every moment of it. I knew how much my twins meant to her—especially Rose—and I saw the pain in her eyes as it dawned on her that they no longer were the young children who lapped up all her attention eagerly.

I stayed for about half an hour longer with her discussing the picnic, and then I returned to the penthouse.

Once the twins are gone, we'll all have much more important things to discuss than birthday parties.

Chapter 2: Rose

"He could wear my grandma's pants and still look sexy," Becky said, looking longingly at my brother who was sitting across the lawn with a group of friends.

"I love that he's growing his hair out a bit," Jessica said, staring at him dreamily, her chin resting in her palms. "Damn, it looks good."

"Seriously, what do your parents feed him?" Silvia asked, turning toward me.

"The same as me," I muttered, rolling my eyes at my friends.

"Who do you think he'll date next, now that he's no longer going out with Yasmine?" Jessica asked.

"No idea."

"Does he still do martial arts training with your dad?" Becky asked.

"Yeah," I said, stretching my legs out on the grass and yawning. "My dad makes us both do it."

"Ahh... Prince Benjamin Novak," Silvia whispered, sighing. "When will you be mine?"

I looked at the three friends who had stayed back with me after the picnic just so they could continue to ogle my brother. Ben was the heartthrob of all the girls on the island. Whenever I was with them while Ben was around, it felt like I might as well not exist.

It was my birthday as well as Ben's, yet throughout the whole picnic my friends had done almost nothing but stare at and gossip about my brother. Occasionally I found myself wondering how many of them were friends with me just so they could get the inside scoop on my brother.

I, on the other hand, didn't seem to get as much attention from the boys my age. Sure, I caught them looking at me, but it was rarely more than that. My girlfriends thought that maybe I intimidated them, being princess of The Shade. My theory was that they were intimidated by the males in my family. I thought that perhaps the prospect of having both Derek and Ben Novak breathing down his neck was just too daunting for a young man to bother. Because my brother was just as protective of me as my father. There were after all lots of other pretty girls on the island with less barriers to entry.

I couldn't say that any of this bothered me much though. My life didn't revolve around finding a boyfriend as my friends' seemed to.

I didn't know if it was just my imagination, but my girlfriends' gossiping seemed to have become worse in recent months and I found myself spending more and more time with Griffin. When he wasn't around, I'd got into the habit of hanging out with my parents' friends instead. I realized that I had more in common with them than most of my contemporaries, who were all still human.

The Shade was an odd place. Although most of my parents' friends were technically in their late teens and early twenties, many had been alive for hundreds of years. In a sense, I got the best of both worlds when I spent time with them. They were still young at heart, yet had so much experience – with centuries' worth of knowledge and stories to share.

"Would you do that for us, Rose?"

I looked up to see my three friends staring at me.

I'd drifted off into my own thoughts and completely lost track of their conversation.

"Sorry, what?" I mumbled.

"We want you to give us a tour of your brother's bedroom," Jessica said, her chestnut brown eyes wide with expectation.

"Oh," I snorted. "No. Trust me. You don't want that. It's such a mess, you have no…"

My voice trailed off as I spotted Anna and Kyle taking a seat on the lawn a few feet away from us with their children, Ariana and Jason.

Although Ariana was four years younger than me, I knew that she would make for better company than my friends right now. I stood up and shook the grass off my dress.

"I'll see you guys around," I muttered, waving a hand and walking away before they could object.

All four looked up as I approached.

"Happy birthday, princess." Kyle grinned. "You want to sit with us?"

"Thanks."

I plopped myself down next to Ariana. Everyone on the island joked that we were twin sisters because our features were similar.

"Happy birthday," Ariana said through a mouthful of cake. "What's up?"

"Ah, nothing much." I sighed, leaning back and looking around the lawn once again. Most of the attendees of our picnic had left by now, with just a few latecomers stopping by to drop gifts off for us and pick up some lunch. "I wanted to thank you so much for the gifts."

"You liked them?" Jason asked, poking his head around Ariana's shoulder to look at me. The ten year old's mouth was covered with strawberry icing.

Anna had knitted pajamas for Ben and I, and they truly were works of art. I hated to think how many hours she must have spent on them.

"They're the most beautiful pajamas I've ever seen," I said, ruffling Jason's hair. "Thank you."

"You're welcome, darling." Anna smiled.

"Hi Rose."

I swivelled around to see who had spoken.

A tall red haired boy with warm hazelnut eyes. And now possibly the best friend I had on the island: Griffin.

"Sorry I couldn't make it earlier," he said, grinning sheepishly.

"Oh, that's fine."

He had one hand hidden behind his back, while he reached the other down to pull me to my feet.

I turned back to Ariana and her family.

"Sorry, guys," I said. "I'll catch you later. Enjoy the rest of your cake."

"Bye!"

I turned back to Griffin and attempted to see what he was

hiding. He stepped away, blocking my view.

"Wait," he said, laughing. "Not yet. Follow me."

He placed his hand on the small of my back and pushed me forward toward the entrance of the woods.

"Where are we going?" I asked, looking over my shoulder and narrowing my eyes on him in mock suspicion.

"Just trust me," he said, still smiling. "It's a surprise."

He led me forward, refusing to answer any of my questions until we reached the Port. We stepped onto the jetty and he walked me right up to its edge.

"Keep your eyes forward," he said.

I placed my hands on the banister and stared out at the dark ocean. I heard a clinking behind me and then Griffin said, "Okay, you can look now."

He stood beside me, holding out a gorgeous shell necklace.

"Happy birthday."

"Oh my." I gasped, reaching out to take the necklace from him.

"I'll put it on you. It's quite delicate."

"Yeah, good idea," I muttered.

I bunched up all my hair above my head and he reached his hands around my neck, fastening the hook.

"I wish there was a mirror here... Did you make this yourself?"

"Yup."

"It's beautiful. Thanks man," I said, giving him a high five. "Since when did ol' Griff start getting in touch with his feminine side?"

"Since I realized I should probably start giving the princess better gifts than home made chocolate pigs every year… which my mom made, by the way. I just took them from the kitchen and pretended they were from me."

"I always thought those pigs tasted suspiciously good," I said, giggling and shoving him in the shoulder. "What did you get Ben?"

"Oh, the pigs again."

"So the princess was deserving of a better gift, but the prince wasn't?"

"Yeah, I guess," he said nonchalantly, reaching a hand behind his head and running it through his hair. "Maybe I'll think of something better for him next year. But for now, it's pigs."

"I see," I said. "And why did you need to bring me all the way here to give me the necklace?"

"Oh, I dunno. Just thought the setting matched the gift." He averted his eyes to the ocean and placed his hands on the banister next to mine. He cleared his throat. "Rose, uh. I also wanted to ask you if…if you—"

"If I still want the pigs too?" I asked, grinning up at him.

He chuckled and shook his head.

"No, actually. I mean, you can have them too if you want but... I-I wanted to ask if you—"

"Rose!"

I whirled around to see Ben emerging from the woods.

"Just a moment, Griff," I said, looking at him apologetically.

"O-okay. Yeah. Sure."

I ran over to my brother.

"Now's the best time to do it," Ben whispered hurriedly. "Almost everyone has gone, but Corrine is still there with Ibrahim."

"Okay," I said, casting a glance back at Griffin. "Just let me say good bye to Griffin."

I left Ben and ran back over to my friend.

"Griff, I've got to go."

I wrapped my arms around his neck and drew him in for a tight hug. As I placed a kiss on his cheek, I felt taken aback to see him blushing.

Feeling awkward, I took a step back. *It's not like I've never hugged him before. What's up with Griff?* I didn't have time to ponder over it, however, since Ben was waiting impatiently for me.

"I've really got to start, uh, packing for my trip. But thank you again for such a stunning and thoughtful gift. You'd better keep up the handiwork though, because I'll expect a crown next year…"

"All right, princess." He smirked, slipping his hands into his pockets. "The necklace does look beautiful on you."

"Thank you…" There was an odd silence between us as he stared at me. "Oh yeah, what was it that you wanted to say to me?"

"Oh, it was nothing," he said quickly. "Really, I've even forgotten what I was going to say."

His cheeks were still a bright red color.

"Oh, okay. Well, if I don't manage to see you again before I leave, I guess I'll see you when I get back in a couple of months."

"Sure thing."

I patted him on the shoulder and ran back over to Ben. We rushed through the woods together until we arrived at the lawn.

I scanned the area for my parents. They appeared to be deeply engrossed in a conversation with Vivienne and Xavier.

Certain that they wouldn't notice me, I left Ben's side and walked over to Corrine, who was still sitting on the grass next to Ibrahim. I took her hand in mine and tugged on her to get up.

"What is it?" she asked.

"I need to talk to you in private," I said.

Corrine looked surprised, but followed me. I led her away from the field and into the woods. I didn't stop walking until we'd reached the Sanctuary, and refused to offer any explanations along the way.

Once we were safely inside her bedroom, I reached into my coat pocket and pulled out two passports, laying them on the table in front of her.

She raised a brow at me. "Rose, what?"

I cleared my throat.

"I told you to wait before giving me a birthday present this year, because I had something specific in mind."

"Yes, and?"

I flipped open Ben's and my passports and pointed to the date of birth inscribed on each of them.

"I want you to work a little magic on these dates," I said.

Her eyes widened.

"Huh?"

"I want you to change them. Set them back."

"Why?"

I sighed.

"My mom keeps saying that this will be our last summer away. Our last summer as normal, human teenagers. Well, if that's the case, I don't want to spend it wallowing around in mud."

"Rose." She looked at me sternly. "Nobody is forcing this

to be your last summer as humans. You don't have to turn into vampires."

"I know, Corrine. I know. But we do want to turn into vampires. We just really wanted this last summer to be special before we do."

She frowned at me, biting her lower lip.

"Well, what exactly do you want to do?"

"This place we're going is off the coast of Scotland. And we'll likely be the youngest there. If we make friends, we want to be able to go to the mainland and stay out late partying. We'll need ID to get into clubs. I was reading in the brochure that people above the age of eighteen are allowed to come and go as they please."

"That's all you want these passports for?"

I nodded.

"All you need to do is change these dates," I said. "Oh, and don't tell my parents about it because I doubt they'd approve."

"What age do you want to be?"

"Twenty-one."

She looked at me dubiously.

"Why twenty-one?"

"It's the legal drinking age in the UK," I lied, praying Corrine wouldn't know any better or verify my statement.

"Hm. You don't exactly look twenty-one."

"Maybe not," I said, "But they're not going to question it if they see it on our ID."

"Hmm... And this is really all you want for your birthday?"

I nodded vigorously.

A small smile curled at the corner of her lips as she reached for the passports and slid them across the table toward her.

"You're making me into a criminal by asking me to tamper with these, you do realize that, don't you? Wait here."

I waited as she left the room. When she returned a few minutes later, she handed me the two passports—the dates changed and looking as though they had been that way all along.

I wrapped my arms around her neck and kissed her cheek.

"Thank you, Aunty Corrine."

She frowned at me.

"I feel awful going behind your parents' backs like this. Just promise me that you won't get yourselves into trouble."

"I promise," I said, grinning and dashing out of the room.

*****

Ben was waiting for me in his room when I returned to the penthouse. He raised his eyebrows expectantly and stood up from the bed.

"Well? Did she give them to you?"

I nodded and handed the passports over for him to inspect.

"And you?" I asked. "Did you do it?"

"Yes, I called them," he replied, reaching into his pocket and pulling out a black mobile phone—one of the few phones on the island that Corrine had charmed to allow outside contact with the world. "Jake says we're still welcome. They were planning to spend the summer in their dad's condo anyway. And he says Kristal is looking forward to seeing you."

I sat down on the bed next to him.

"Good. So that's accommodation sorted. Now, let's count the money... and we also need to think about plane tickets," I muttered.

Ben reached under his bed. He pulled out a leather pouch stuffed full of cash. We both started counting up all the pocket money we'd been given by our parents and grandfather over the years that we hadn't had an opportunity to spend. It amounted to several thousand dollars. Certainly more than enough for two months, especially considering that accommodation would be free of charge.

"So, here's how this is going to work," I said, once we'd tucked all the money back into Ben's pouch and replaced it beneath his bed. I rubbed my temples as I tried to think the plan through. "Corrine will drop us off on the little Scottish island. It will be in the evening, so we may as well spend the night there. But the next morning, we'll catch a boat out of there and head toward the nearest airport. The staff at the island won't bat an eyelid on seeing us leave because we'll have checked in as twenty-one-year-olds with these passports. So, we'll arrive at the airport. We'll pay for tickets in cash and book the first flights out of there."

Ben nodded. "And we'll take this phone with us as we usually do. They've never tried calling the camps we've stayed at before—they've always contacted us directly on the mobile. So they're never going to know we're not in Scotland."

Ben and I stared at each other as the scale of the trick we were about to attempt settled upon us like a heavy weight.

The truth was, I didn't enjoy lying to my parents. And Ben didn't either. Yes, Ben and I threw our strops, but at the end of the day we didn't like to see worry written all over their faces.

But the invitation of our friends from last summer camp—Kristal and Jake—had begun ringing in our ears as soon as our mother had mentioned we were to be going on this stupid adventure course. That, and the fact that this really was going to be our last summer as humans.

"It's just this once," Ben said quietly. "For two months. They'll never know. We'll just make sure to be back in Scotland on the date Corrine is due to pick us up."

I nodded, though his words didn't dissipate the guilt that had settled in my stomach. We had never perpetrated such a massive deception before. We'd be betraying not only our parents' trust, but also Corrine's.

I stood up and walked around the room, breathing deeply.

"Well," I muttered. "Hawaii, here we come."

Chapter 3: Derek

Once Corrine had left the island with Ben and Rose, the first thing I did was call a council meeting in the Great Dome.

Sofia and I sat at the head of the long table, Vivienne and Xavier either side of us. The room filled up with our most trusted comrades.

Once everyone had seated themselves, I cleared my throat and began.

"So, our children have turned seventeen. As you all know, Sofia and I vowed that we wouldn't get entangled with any situation that was risky until this time." I looked down at Sofia.

She nodded, reassuring me.

"Over the past decade, these beach kidnappings have remained steady, while the police have remained clueless. It should be apparent by now that there is likely some greater force at work than humans."

"May I ask what these kidnappings have to do with us?" Claudia called out.

My eyes settled on the blonde vampire.

"If our suspicions are correct that these kidnappings are not being done by humans, then we ought to know who is behind them. Especially since they are going on so close to our own turf."

I paused to look around the room.

"Also," Sofia said, "I say that since we have knowledge of this hidden world of supernaturals—something normal people could never have—we ought to use this knowledge to get to the bottom of this. It's our responsibility. Nobody else will solve this mystery unless we do."

Her words sounded strange to my ears. Although we'd stopped kidnapping humans and drinking their blood almost two decades ago, this was the first time in centuries that the vampires of The Shade were opening their minds to the possibility that our responsibilities might stretch outside of our own little world.

"So, what's the first step?" Yuri asked.

Eli turned to look at his brother.

"There's only one option. Reach the latest kidnapping spot as soon as possible after the disappearance. I suggest that Ibrahim or another witch vanishes us to the location, and that way we can escape quickly if an official approaches. As I said, we may find nothing... or we may find something. I suggest we bring Shadow, since he has the best senses of all of us."

"So where was the last crime scene?" Landis asked.

"Cancún. A bunch of humans went missing along the beach all on the same evening, leaving no trace of any struggle. According to the reporters, they just vanished."

"Cancún," Sofia repeated, alarmed. "Mexico."

Eli nodded.

"All right," I said. "For now, I suggest just a handful of us go. It'll be easier to appear and then make a hasty exit if need be. Myself, Sofia, Eli and Shadow I think will be a good idea to start with... and a witch."

"I'll come," Ibrahim said.

"That's settled then," I said.

Eli, Sofia and Ibrahim all nodded.

I dismissed everybody. Sofia and I remained seated until the dome was empty. She was breathing deeply and I didn't miss the slight tremble in her hand. I pulled her against my chest. Kissing the top of her head, I said, "I know what you're feeling. But Rose and Ben will learn the truth sooner or later. They've got these last two months of oblivion on their little island. When they come back, we tell them."

Sofia nodded. "I know. And we'll make use of their time away to work on this problem. I-I just…" She stopped short, choking up. "I just don't want anything to happen to them again."

I brushed my thumbs against her cheeks and kissed her forehead.

I wanted to promise her that nothing would ever happen to our twins. I wanted to reassure her that they would never be put in harm's way or threatened ever again.

But I couldn't.

Because I didn't know what the future held. Neither of us did.

Everyone had been expecting Ben and Rose to grow up with some kind of supernatural ability—given my fire powers and Sofia being an immune when they were conceived—but so far they'd shown no sign of it. I knew that this made Sofia more nervous for them. They were just normal, fragile humans.

"Now that they're almost adults," I said, "the best thing we can do for them is arm them with knowledge and train them to stay out of danger."

"I know." She inhaled, her voice deep with resignation. "And to do this, we first need to figure out what kind of danger is surrounding us."

Chapter 4: Rose

The journey went smoother than either of us was expecting.

Corrine left us at the Scottish island without much fuss and we stayed the night there. The next morning, we checked out and took the ferry back to the mainland where we travelled by a combination of bus and train to Glasgow airport. Direct flights weren't available for when we wanted them, so the journey took longer than we had expected, but finally we touched down in Honolulu.

As we passed through arrivals, I spotted Kristal and Jake waiting for us. Kristal was eighteen, while Jake was nineteen. They were both tall, like us—though Ben was still the tallest among us. Being almost six foot already, he was well on track to reach our dad's height. Kristal and Jake both shared the same blond hair and blue eyes.

I looked at Ben for a reaction on seeing Kristal. He scowled and shoved me in the shoulder. "Stop it," he whispered, as we approached.

I rolled my eyes.

"Hey, you guys!" Kristal squealed. She ducked beneath the barrier and wrapped her arms around me, kissing either cheek. Ben's cheeks flushed ever so slightly as she did the same to him.

"Hi, Rose."

I looked up to see Jake staring down at me.

"Hi, Jake," I said.

I gave him a quick hug and kissed either cheek politely. He smelled of expensive aftershave.

They led us out of the airport toward a parking lot where we stopped in front of a shiny black limousine. I looked up at Kristal.

"Seriously?"

She beamed. "Hop in."

We all climbed into the back and the car moved forward.

"So this is yours?" I asked.

"Nah, we rented this especially for you as a surprise." Kristal smiled. "Though Andre in the front there *is* my dad's driver."

"You really shouldn't have," Ben said.

"It's our pleasure," she replied, touching Ben on the shoulder.

Kristal and Jake's parents were divorced. Their mother lived in New York, while their father—a wealthy businessman—split his time between Hawaii and San Francisco. Kristal had explained that their father often allowed them to stay in his condo by themselves during the summer.

After about an hour of driving, we pulled up in the underground parking area of a towering block of apartments. We exited the car, heaved our luggage out and took the elevator up to their condo.

I breathed out slowly as Jake pushed the door open and we walked inside. Everything about the place exuded luxury and class. The external walls of the apartment consisted almost entirely of tinted windows. The floors were white marble and looked clean enough to eat off, beige carpets sprawling out at strategic positions. There was a massive flatscreen TV in the sitting room and a black leather couch. It didn't have the homely feel of our penthouse in The Shade, but it was certainly more flashy.

Kristal showed me to my spacious room next door to hers, while Jake led Ben further along the corridor. Once we'd settled in, Kristal ordered some pizza and French fries. We all sat down around the kitchen table to eat.

"So," she said. "Is there anything in particular you'd like to do while you're here?"

"Party," I blurted out, through a mouthful of Pizza Margherita.

"What kind of partying?" Jake asked.

I shrugged.

"Just whatever kind you normally do."

"All right," Kristal said, chewing thoughtfully. "We'll head out to the beachfront at nine. There's a party going on down there tonight, near one of our favorite bars. A few of our friends are supposed to be there too. You could meet them."

"We'll have to buy drinks for you, if you want them," Jake said.

"That won't be necessary." I fetched the passports from my handbag and placed them on the table in front of them, pointing to the dates of birth.

Jake and Kristal's mouths dropped open.

"These are fake passports?" she gasped.

"Just changed the date on the real ones," Ben said. "A friend of ours is, uh, very good with things like this."

They looked at us, stunned.

"Wow," Kristal said. "I might want to get the phone number of that friend."

I laughed nervously and changed the subject as we finished eating. Then Ben and I retreated to our rooms for a nap before the party.

*****

The party was only a few minutes away, so we walked. Ben wore a loose shirt and jeans, similar to what Jake was wearing. Kristal wore a miniskirt, a low-cut blouse and thick high heels designed for the sand, while I wore a flowing summer dress and sandals. High heels made my feet ache and I always felt awkward wearing short skirts and dresses. It gave me constant anxiety that a rogue gust of wind might creep up on me, revealing the color of my panties to the world. I knew that it was stupid, but it was just one of my quirks.

"You're such a dork," Kristal said, laughing, after I told her.

"Maybe." I smirked, nudging her in the shoulder. "But at least I'm a comfortable dork."

Music boomed and lights flashed as we approached the party. Everyone appeared to be young, in their late teens or early twenties. Kristal grabbed my hand and led me deeper into the crowd. I looked around for Ben but I could no longer see even him above the sea of bobbing heads.

Kristal led me until we reached a patch of sand with enough space to breathe. A man came up with a tray of canapés and champagne. I accepted both and thanked him. Kristal just took a glass of champagne.

I finally spotted Ben and Jake approaching us, already holding glasses. My eyes settled on Jake, his white shirt slightly undone at the top. When he made eye contact with me, I hurriedly looked back down at my drink. We stood together awkwardly for a few minutes, sipping from our glasses and glancing around. Eventually I just stared at Ben, since it was more convenient than having to keep thinking of places to look other than Jake. My brother looked down at me and widened his eyes.

"What?" Ben mouthed.

I rolled my eyes and looked down at my toes. Then Kristal moved away from me.

"Well, our friends still haven't arrived," she said loudly over the blaring music. "I guess we may as well start without them. Do you want to dance, Ben?"

I couldn't stop the grin from spreading over across my face as Ben swallowed a mouthful of his drink a little too quickly.

"Yeah," he said. "Sure."

He took her hand, following her to an empty spot a few feet away. She started dancing as soon as they reached it, placing her arms around his shoulders and moving her hips to the beat.

Jake cleared his throat next to me.

Oh.

He looked down at me expectantly, a smile on his lips. He nodded his head toward a spot next to them.

"You want to dance?"

"Uh. O-okay."

He held out his hand and led me toward a spot near Ben and Kristal. Ben threw me an exaggerated wink as soon as he saw me. I rolled my eyes.

"What's wrong?"

Jake was looking down at me, frowning.

Crap.

"I-I was just making a face at Ben."

"Okay," Jake said, smiling now—though he still looked a little disconcerted. "Because if I'm boring you and you'd rather dance with someone else, just say."

"No! No. Of course not!" I blurted out the words so quickly it made the situation feel even more awkward.

My cheeks blazed.

I felt uncomfortable dancing. The girls in skimpy dresses all around me were dancing like they'd been born in a club. I felt clumsy and out of place in my flowing dress and brown sandals.

Sandals. What were you thinking, Rose? I was shocked to find myself wishing that I'd borrowed one of Kristal's short dresses.

I tried to concentrate on the rhythm and beat of the music. But the music felt so foreign to me, it was hard to flow with it. The more I tried, the more I pictured myself as the Tin Man from *The Wizard of Oz*.

Ben and I had been exposed to music aplenty. But not this type of music—club music. Stuff that people our age listened to.

Our father had encouraged Ben and I to take up musical instruments from a young age. I'd played both the harp and piano since I was six years old, while Ben played the piano and guitar. Our dad had taught us both. But our dad's taste in music was rather old-fashioned, as one would expect from a man born in the fifteenth century.

"They've arrived!" Jake shouted over the music, pointing toward a group of girls and boys our age who'd just broken through the crowd. He let go of me and walked toward a tall, skinny blonde girl in a black glittery minidress and heels so high they made my feet ache just looking at them.

He wrapped his arms around her waist and reached down to kiss her on the lips.

Oh.

I see.

Kristal's newly arrived friends all dressed and danced like goddesses. Just like Kristal herself and apparently every other girl on this beach except me.

Jake pulled the blonde toward an empty patch of sand and she started gyrating against him. All the other boys seemed to have arrived with partners.

Ben was still dancing with Kristal. She hadn't left him as Jake had left me. And he was coping better than I was with the music. Much better. Then again, Kristal was doing most of the dancing against him; he just had to follow along with her, supporting her moves. He looked like pretty much any other guy in the party.

"I'm going to take a break." I didn't know why I said it out loud, since nobody could have possibly heard me.

I thought back to the brochure my mother had given me of that Scottish survival course.

Maybe I would have been better suited wallowing around in one of those mud pools.

I walked over to the bar and, flashing my passport, picked up another glass of champagne. I sat down in the corner in view of the dance area and downed it in one gulp. The bubbles shot up my nose and I descended into a coughing fit. Thanks to the music, nobody noticed except for the bartender. I stood up and picked up another drink from the counter.

Or maybe I just need to be drunker. All these girls seem pretty drunk. Maybe that's how they dance so well.

I downed one glass after the other until my head felt lighter, and my discomfort started to dull. But when I looked around the party again, I couldn't spot any guy free who was good-looking enough for me to want to approach.

I waited for about half an hour, sitting and looking around hopefully. But the only men who looked available appeared older. Much older.

The heavy electro music reverberating around the party was starting to make my eardrums hurt. I walked toward the border of the dance area and turned around to glance back at Ben and Kristal. When neither noticed that I'd even moved from my place, I split from the crowd. Removing my sandals, I walked onto the sand toward the dark ocean. I breathed in deeply and approached the waves, dipping my feet in.

I think I can dance now. I just need to find someone...

Oh, my.

Almost as soon as the thought entered my head, a dozen young-looking guys walked along the beach toward the party. There were no girls in sight.

My eyes fixed on the young man at the front. He looked around Jake's age, maybe slightly older.

He is... handsome. Very. Handsome.

He wore black jeans and a smart navy shirt. He was tall—several inches taller than Ben—and well built, the muscles in his arms flexing as he walked. His strong jawline was covered with just enough stubble to give him a rugged, sexy look, while his dark hair brushed the sides of his face. He had deep chocolate-brown eyes.

Quick, Rose. Move!

Flinging my sandals into the waves, I raced toward him barefoot across the sand.

"Hey, you," I said, stumbling in front of the young man before he could enter the dance area. I stared up at him, panting. He looked even hotter now that I was closer to him. My breathing became heavier. "D-dance with me."

I held out my hand.

His eyes locked on mine. Then he took a step back and I watched as he looked me over from head to foot.

I thought for a moment that he was going to refuse, but then, wordlessly, he took my hand and pulled me toward the dance area. His hand felt cold for such warm weather.

I hiked up the end of my gown and attempted to fashion it into a shorter dress by tying some of the excess fabric around my waist. I glanced around at the other girls once more as I prepared to unleash my newfound moves. But before I could start, he caught hold of my waist and began to lead the way, guiding my every movement.

I didn't even need to think. I just had to move where he was positioning me.

Oh, this is much easier.

Why couldn't Jake have just done this?

This guy was good. He was making *me* look good.

I glanced around at the crowd until I finally caught Ben's eye. I gave him a huge wink.

He laughed and got Kristal's attention. Kristal, her cheeks pink and forehead shining with sweat, looked over the stranger I was dancing with and gave me a thumbs up.

Okay, now we're finally back on track to this being a good night.

"How did you learn to dance so well?" I shouted into the stranger's ear.

"I dance a lot." His voice was deep and husky.

"Oh," I said.

I couldn't think of further conversation. But it didn't feel awkward not talking, because he kept me moving and barely even gave me a chance to talk even if I had wanted to.

I found it a little disconcerting the way he kept looking around at the other men he'd arrived with as we were dancing. I thought that perhaps he was checking out the girls they'd hooked up with. I looked around myself. Each of them seemed to have found partners by now.

He bent down and whispered into my ear, "Care to take a walk outside?"

"Yeah," I slurred. "Sure."

He gripped my hand and led me away from the crowd. It was getting hot and the cool sea air felt welcome. His muscular arm wrapped around my waist as we walked along the sand.

"So," I said, looking up at his face. "What's your name?"

"Caleb."

"Caleb," I repeated. I liked the sound of his name rolling off my tongue, so I said it again. "Caaaa-leb."

We walked side by side for about fifteen more minutes, the disco music and lights draining in the distance, until we were approaching a quiet part of the beach. When I looked around, I found it strange that his friends had all left at the same time with their girls, and we were all walking in the same direction.

Even in my drunk state, I found this odd. I stopped in my tracks. It was only now in the natural light of the full moon that I noticed just how pale his face was.

My breath hitched.

I'd seen enough vampires in my life. There were small differences in the formation of the upper jawbone— extremely subtle, but noticeable.

"A-are you a vampire?"

I felt crazy saying the words out loud. But his eyes widened and he took a step back from me. "What?"

"I've never seen you before in The Shade, but—"

"The Shade?"

He gripped my arms so tightly it hurt, his deep brown eyes narrowing on me.

"Who are you?" he whispered, barely breathing.

"Rose Novak. My parents are—"

Before I could even finish my sentence, he swore and let go of me with such force that I stumbled onto the sand.

He called out to the other men, "Do it now! We need to leave!"

The men pulled out needles from their pockets all at once, and in a whir of motion, the girls lay limp in their arms. They all ran into the ocean, carrying their victims over their shoulders. I could barely shout out before a black submarine emerged from the waters. They piled in through the hatch.

Caleb glared down at me and, without another word, raced into the water and leapt through the hatch after them.

Seconds later, the submarine was gone.

Chapter 5: Rose

Ben didn't believe me last night when I told him. He said that I was just drunk out of my mind and hauled me back to the condo, leaving Kristal and Jake to continue partying until dawn.

Only when we switched on the local news the following morning to find out that almost a dozen girls had gone missing from that beach that very night did he start to take notice of what I was saying.

He pulled me into his room and shut the door.

"So you're telling me that vampires are responsible for this?"

"Yes," I said irritably, rubbing my head as I tried to relieve my hangover. "I saw a group of vampires steal them away. The guy—Caleb, his name was—would have stolen me away too if I hadn't told him that I was a Novak."

Ben heaved a sigh and sat down on the bed next to me, resting his own head in his hands.

"And you are sure that you didn't recognize any of these vampires from The Shade?"

"No way." I shook my head, recalling how hot Caleb was. "Trust me, I would have remembered them."

"Then who the hell are they? And why are they going around stealing people?"

I paused and continued to massage my temples with my fingers.

"Ben, we should call Mom and Dad to tell them about this."

He stared at me.

"You do realize that if we do that, our two months of freedom will be over before they've even begun?"

"Obviously. But what other option do we have?"

"What would Mom and Dad do about this even if they knew?"

Ben had a point. We couldn't dictate that another coven should live without human blood like everyone did in The Shade. Drinking human blood was just a part of life for most vampires—no different than humans eating animals for their flesh.

I supposed that I would have been more horrified by the thought of all those girls being kidnapped had I not grown up all my life around vampires. Although the vampires of The Shade no longer fed on humans, it was part of their nature to crave human blood and I knew that it was a daily struggle for The Shade's vampires to exercise restraint and sustain themselves only on animal blood. It was rather macabre to realize how desensitized I was to the situation.

"I suppose there's not much they could do about it," I began slowly. "Though I still think that we should tell them when we return. Mom and Dad have never mentioned any other covens still existing today except for our own. They always told us that the other vampires were taken back through the portal into Cruor—and those who weren't joined us in The Shade. It's really very odd."

"Okay, I agree," Ben said. "We'll tell them when we get back."

There was a knock on the door. Ben got up to open it and Kristal walked into the room in her bathrobe.

"How did you both sleep?" she asked.

I rubbed my throbbing head and muttered, "Good."

"You really scored last night," she said, sitting down on the bed next to me and squeezing my knee.

"Yeah." I sighed. "I did."

Chapter 6: Aiden

As I approached the front door of Yuri and Claudia's penthouse, my hands trembled. Exhaling deeply, I reached for the front door but paused just before I knocked.

Pressing my head against the door, I shut my eyes tight.

What am I doing?

I'd been feeling crazy ever since I seriously began to entertain Sofia's suggestion that I turned, but now I felt downright bonkers.

Do I really want to become the creature that killed my father? That ripped my family apart? How will I even look myself in the mirror?

I'd spent enough time around the vampires of The Shade for my prejudices that all these creatures were the same to disappear. But some things that were associated with the pale bloodsuckers—like the horrific images from my past—just couldn't be undone.

But then my darling Sofia had turned into one. Along with Derek. And they even spoke of turning their children once they were old enough to make an informed decision. And something had stirred within me. A desire to live on past my natural lifetime. I felt blessed to have the family that I had, and somehow, my limited human lifespan didn't feel enough. Knowing that they would go on to live eternally while I passed away after a few more decades was haunting.

Sofia didn't stop urging me either.

So here I stood.

So this is the day Aiden, one of the most feared hunters the world has ever known, becomes the very creature he hunted.

Clearing my throat, I knocked on the door.

Footsteps sounded and the short blonde vampire appeared in the doorway.

"Oh, Yuri," she called. "Look who's here for your, ahem, services."

She winked at me and opened the door fully for me to step inside.

Yuri entered the hallway and, rolling his eyes at her, walked up to me and gripped my hand in a firm shake.

"You'll have to excuse my wife," Yuri said, eyeing Claudia with mock disdain. "As much as I've tried over the years, I still haven't quite managed to rescue her mind from the gutter."

Claudia reached up and grabbed Yuri's ear between her fingers, yanking him down to her level to kiss him full on the mouth.

"Baby," she whispered as their lips parted. "Stop pretending you'd want me any other way."

Yuri's cheeks flushed. He pulled away from her and stood up straight, clearing his throat.

"I'll leave you two to it," she said, winking and floating out of the room.

"Well," Yuri said, raising his eyes to me and grinning sheepishly. "Follow me through here."

I followed him into their spare bedroom, which he had stripped of all furniture, curtains and carpets. Anything that could be stained with blood or ruined in case I was overcome by a violent fit, as was often the case with newly turned vampires.

"You sure you want me to be the one to do this?" he asked, eyeing me dubiously.

Yuri had come to be my best friend on that island—the level of friendship I'd struck up with the young vampire had surprised even me. Somehow, I felt more comfortable with him turning me than my own daughter. I didn't know what state I would *wake up in, and exposing my daughter to that side of me before I got control of myself made me very uncomfortable. I trusted Yuri and developed a level of comfort of him over the years that I felt I could discuss things with him—man to man—that I felt embarrassed discussing with others. He just seemed to be the logical choice, the first person to spring to mind, when I thought about who should turn me.*

I nodded and lay down on the wooden table in the center of the room.

"Let's just get this over with," I said, grimacing.

"All right. Man, this ain't gonna be pretty."

*****

Splashing cold water over my face, I looked up at myself in my bathroom mirror. Even after eleven years of being a bloodsucker, my reflection still shocked me sometimes.

Those first few years had been harrowing. That all-consuming greed to feed on human blood. To hunt, to harm, to devour. I hadn't allowed myself to even go near the part of the island where my grandchildren lived for the first month after turning. The whole experience had made me more sympathetic toward vampires than I could have ever been before.

Somehow, it had also given me renewed emotional strength.

The day I'd pushed my wife into the pit knowing she'd be burnt alive, I'd thought my ability to feel for anyone else ever again had burned alongside her.

Then along came Adelle. The shy, soft-spoken witch who through her devotion to teaching the children of The Shade soon became appointed headmistress.

The striking red-haired beauty had called to me like a siren the moment I'd laid eyes on her. But I'd still felt too numb inside to do anything about it.

But then, when I'd turned… something had shifted inside me. Perhaps it was a renewal of confidence. Confidence to open up again in ways that I hadn't thought I was capable of while still a human. I supposed that confidence was a natural consequence of knowing you'd live forever.

My daughter had encouraged me ever since I'd first turned. *"You've got forever now, Dad. You need to find someone to live it with other than just me and the kids."*

I'd come to realize that I'd been through enough heartbreak and pain in my mortal life already for much more to make a difference, especially since I now had an eternity to recover from it.

I took a shower and got dressed. Although I dressed casually, inwardly, my stomach was in knots as I prepared myself for what I was about to do. Today was a big day. The day that I was going to ask a girl out on a date. The day I would hopefully escape the dreaded friend zone, as Sofia would have referred to it.

I hadn't told Sofia yet that I was pursuing Adelle. Sofia would find out if and when we became lovers. I smiled as I imagined the smile on Sofia's face if it actually happened.

Leaving my penthouse, I headed toward the Vale and stopped once I reached the town square, in clear view of the entrance to the school where I was due to meet Adelle.

I had to catch myself from exhaling too audibly as she stepped out onto the steps. Her long wavy hair hung loose down her shoulders, and she wore a pretty floral summer dress that stopped just above her knees.

"Aiden! There you are."

"Hi, Adelle."

She walked up to me and greeted me with a peck on the cheek.

"Shall we?" I held out my arm for her to grasp and led her away from the clearing and into the forest.

"Well, I'm intrigued, to say the least, about what you might want with me on this fine summer's evening."

"I thought it'd be nice to take a walk after school for a change, rather than always chatting in the classrooms."

We walked through the forest making small talk. I stopped once we reached the old boathouse on the border of the lake. I led her inside and to the edge of the wall, where the windows were open, affording us full view of the beauty of the lake. The scent of fragrant lotuses drifted up toward us.

"Even in the darkness, it's so beautiful here in the summer," she remarked. "I always look forward to this time of year."

"Don't you miss your real home? The Sanctuary? I've heard that the witches' realm is ten times more beautiful than this."

She leaned her arms over the banister and stared down at the water, gathering her thick hair so it fell down one shoulder.

"Everything is superficially beautiful there," she said. "Me? I like raw beauty. Everything feels real, genuine, on this island. And the people. Oh, the people here. They have heart. Something that's rare to find back where I come from."

"And it's all worth it even with a shortened lifespan?"

"That's a myth, in my opinion. I've seen no evidence of witches aging faster on Earth than they do back in The Sanctuary. We can stay youthful for hundreds, sometimes even thousands of years… depending on how we look after ourselves, of course."

I stared at her lovely face and wondered how old she really was, but dared not ask.

"Do you ever regret your decision to turn into a vampire?" she asked, looking up at me seriously.

I gazed down into her light blue eyes.

"I never thought I'd say this, but I don't. Not a bit. The first few years were rough, yes. But now, it's all been worth it."

"Well, I for one am glad that you turned," she said softly. "It would have been sad to lose you."

We stared at each other for a few moments before I finally gathered enough courage to stop procrastinating.

"Adelle, listen," I said, taking her hands in mine. "I wanted to ask you something—"

Ring. Ring. Ring.

The phone in my pocket began vibrating.

Oh, bloody hell.

Since Derek and Sofia had left the island with Eli and Ibrahim, I'd been entrusted with the phone in case the twins called.

"I-I'm so sorry," I said. "Just a moment."

Adelle withdrew her hands from mine. I turned away from her and flipped open the phone. "Hello?"

"Hey, this is Ben."

"Hi, Ben."

"Where's Mom and Dad?"

"They're not around. They've... gone out for the day."

"Oh, okay. Well, I'm just calling to let you know that Scotland is actually awesome."

"Oh. That's good."

"It's so much better than it looked in the brochure."

"Uh-huh."

"Seriously, great job booking this place."

"Mm-hmm."

"And we're doing just fine. No need to worry about us at all. We've already made friends."

"Well, that's great to hear, Ben."

"So tell Mom and Dad when they get back that we're having fun and they don't need to worry about us. We'll call again in a few days."

"Will do."

"Cool. Bye, Grandpa!"

I flipped the phone shut as Ben hung up.

Grandpa. I winced at the word. As much as I adored being a grandfather to such beautiful children, this was the one moment in my life when I didn't want to be reminded of the fact.

I glanced over at Adelle, slipping the phone back into my pocket.

"It was just Ben," I said, as though she hadn't been in earshot of the entire conversation.

She blushed and smiled. "You're so good with them."

"Yeah," I muttered, averting my eyes to the floor and kicking around a twig. "I suppose I am."

"So, um. What was it that you wanted to say to me?"

"Oh… I just wanted to thank you for doing such a good job with my, uh, grandchildren."

Keep digging, Gramps. Keep digging.

"Oh," she said. She looked surprised—perhaps even disappointed—by my response. "You're more than welcome. They've always been an absolute pleasure to teach."

Now sit back and enjoy the view of that perfect moment blowing right out of the window, asshole…

Chapter 7: Rose

Ben and I made excuses to avoid the beach when it was dark from then on. We spent many daylight hours there, soaking up the sun and swimming in the sea. But when we went out late at night, we made sure that we went to clubs and restaurants further inland.

Unfortunately, I didn't meet another boy like Caleb.

But after several nights of practice—and Kristal giving me some extra sessions during the day around the condo—I was beginning to feel a bit less of a klutz. Kristal had been surprised that I seemed so disorientated listening to modern music and asked me if I really had never gone to a party before. I explained to her that I'd just always been bad at dancing.

I also went shopping with Kristal to buy some new clothes and a pair of high heels. Despite Kristal pressuring me, I still didn't cave into buying miniskirts or minidresses. I did make a compromise, however: the dresses that I came home were all shorter than my long summer gowns—they stopped just above the knee, and I felt confident wearing them.

One evening, there was a big boxing match on the TV, followed immediately by soccer, that Jake didn't want to miss, so Ben decided to stay in with him.

Kristal was excited about the idea of a girls' night out. "We'll go out for dinner together," she said, pulling me into her room and sitting me down in front of her dressing table. "Let me do your hair and makeup."

I'd gotten used to the fact that she always liked to dress me up before going out. It was for my own benefit, since she always made me look better than I could. I wasn't used to wearing makeup. I'd never had much occasion to around The Shade.

Kristal began tugging at my long dark hair with a brush, taming it into a slick ponytail. Then she took out her makeup box and set about giving me what she called a "smoky eye" look.

Smoky or not, I had to admit when I looked in the mirror that it suited me. And once I'd changed into one of my new dresses, fastened Griffin's necklace around my neck and pulled on a pair of heels, I felt thoroughly sexy. I even caught Jake eyeing me as we made our way out through the front door.

Just as we were about to enter the elevator, Kristal stopped abruptly.

"Oh, damn it. Wait here. I forgot something."

She ran back to the apartment and returned a minute later carrying a small black handbag.

"This is Chloe's," Kristal explained. "She left it with me when we were all out the other night and I forgot to return it to her."

We exited the building and, to my discomfort, she turned right—toward the beach. She picked up her mobile phone and dialed a number.

"Chloe? Hi, you're at Jacob's right now? Okay, don't go anywhere because I'm coming with your bag."

Hurrying alongside her, I felt a sinking feeling in my stomach. We reached the beach and stopped once we reached Jacob's Restaurant. Chloe, a short brunette, sat next to her boyfriend, John. Kristal walked over and handed her the bag. They were sitting at a table outside in the open air, with a clear view onto the beach.

We were about to leave when Chloe said, "Hey, why don't you join us? There's plenty of room and we haven't even started eating yet."

Kristal answered before even consulting me.

"That sounds like a great idea," she said.

I didn't argue since it would have been too awkward. I took a seat next to Kristal, opposite Chloe and John across the table.

I tried to convince myself that I was being paranoid. Yes, it was night. And yes, we were sitting right on the beach. But we were near a restaurant, and that was probably the worst kind of place to collect humans, with everybody seated at tables. No way to mingle with drunk crowds.

Still, I failed to relax as we sat for hours on the beachfront, so close to where those girls had been abducted. I found myself looking suspiciously at each person who walked by us.

"Are you all right, Rose?" Kristal asked, squeezing my knee beneath the table. "You're awfully quiet."

"Yes, I'm fine," I muttered. "I'm just a little tired."

"We can go back home now if you want. We don't have to stay for dessert."

"Okay," I said, nodding and clutching her hand. "Let's do that."

Kristal called for the bill and insisted on paying for all of us.

We all got up to leave together and I breathed a sigh of relief as we bade goodbye to the couple and left the beach.

I was so focussed on getting back to our apartment that I didn't think to check if anyone was following us.

If I had, I would have noticed two tall, dark figures trailing in the shadows behind us.

Chapter 8: Sofia

Walking along that Cancún beach that evening after the sun went down was chilling. It looked uncannily similar to the beach I'd been kidnapped from by Lucas all those years ago.

That evening when it all began.

I fantasized briefly about what might have happened had Benjamin Hudson, my best friend, not forgotten it was my birthday that day.

Would none of this have happened? Would I not be standing next to Derek now?

I smiled bitterly as I felt the sand beneath my bare feet. Memories of Ben came flooding back through my mind. That handsome, perfect, blond blue-eyed boy who had once held my heart within the palm of his hand. I could almost feel the exact emotions I'd felt that evening when he'd let me down on my birthday yet again. All because of that cheerleader, Tanya Wilson.

If only you had known then, Sofia, how stupid those feelings would seem now.

That used to be all my world consisted of—Ben and my pain over his latest girlfriend. My pining for his attention.

Derek must have detected what was going through my mind, because he wrapped an arm around me and placed a tender kiss on my forehead. I looked out at the deep dark ocean, fighting to hold back the tears.

Where are you now, Ben?

If only you could see what a beautiful young woman Abby has blossomed into.

If only you could be here with us now.

If only you could have found a love of your own to give you the strength to fight the battle you could have won...

It still haunted me to this day, the way he had just given up on his life. Had he just allowed us to feed him the blood from Derek's palm in those crucial few moments that his soul was still one with his body, he might have been with us now. No matter how hard I tried to understand, I still felt defeated by it. He'd had so much to live for. Yet he'd given it all up willingly, without even a struggle.

I still hadn't forgiven him for it after all these years. And now I doubted that I ever would.

By the time we were halfway along the beach, I'd lost my battle with tears—the memories cutting open my wounds afresh. Wounds that I'd thought had healed years ago.

Derek stopped walking and cradled me against his chest. When Eli and Ibrahim stopped to ask what was wrong, he told them to keep walking.

"I know he's not coming back," I breathed. "And I know it's been years. But, God, it still hurts. It hurts like it was yesterday."

Derek bent down and kissed my cheek, then brushed his own cool cheek against mine and whispered into my ear, "Some scars just don't heal, Sofia. You need to accept that."

I gripped Derek tighter against me.

"Thank you," I gasped, breaking down into a fresh wave of tears. "I-I needed to hear that."

I sank to my knees and he sat with me. I stayed there sobbing in his arms until I felt steady enough to get up and continue walking.

We ran to catch up with Ibrahim, Eli and Shadow.

"I'm sorry," I said, my voice hoarse.

"The last thing you need to do is apologize, Sofia," Eli said.

I gave them a watery smile.

"Okay," I said, drawing in a deep breath. "Let's get down to business."

We walked along the length of the beach that night until we reached the area the humans had disappeared from.

We searched all around, scanned the sand, splashed around in the waves looking for any clue that could tell us what had happened. Shadow was finding nothing of interest to us—although he was certainly finding things that were of interest to him. An orange buoy, a dead whale shark and an unholy amount of seaweed.

Of course, we'd expected not to find anything. After all, if these were supernatural creatures, they wouldn't leave traces.

Once there wasn't any more beach to scan, we all gathered together in a circle and looked at each other. Then all eyes fixed on Eli.

"So?" Ibrahim said.

Eli ran a hand through his hair and heaved a sigh.

"We need to return home and I need to get my maps out."

"And?" Derek said.

"I need to analyze all the locations they've hit over the past few years. I want to see if I can spot any pattern."

"And what if there isn't any pattern?" I asked.

"I agree, it's a long shot," Eli said. "But whoever or whatever is taking these humans has never been caught on any CCTV camera, even after all these years. They—or it—deliberately target wide open areas like this. I don't see what else we can do right now other than try to piece together a pattern. If we are able to spot something, it might give us some clue as to what area they might hit next."

"I suppose it might also give us a clearer guess as to their location," Ibrahim suggested.

Eli nodded. "Because so far, only one thing is apparent. They like their beach parties."

Chapter 9: Rose

The elevator doors were about to close when a gloved hand slipped through. Two men wearing sunglasses entered the elevator and pressed the button for the doors to close.

"Sorry," one of them muttered, as he ran a finger over the floor number we had already pressed.

The elevator being small, I huddled closer to Kristal and looked down at the floor. I always felt awkward standing in elevators with strangers.

The ding sounded once we arrived at level seven and the doors opened. The two men's footsteps followed behind us. When we stopped outside the door, I gripped Kristal's hand before she could open the door with her keys. We stayed standing still, waiting for the footsteps to pass.

They got fainter as they disappeared down the corridor. I breathed out. I released Kristal's hand and she opened the door.

"You sure are jittery tonight," Kristal said as she locked the door behind us.

The television blared from the living room. We left our shoes by the doorway and I sat down on the couch next to the boys, who were munching on popcorn and yelling at the screen. Kristal went into the kitchen and returned later with some fruit tea for us.

"Agh, I can't take any more of this," she said after about two minutes of trying to watch their match. "Let's go into my room."

I followed her and we changed into our pajamas. Then we went into her bathroom. Kristal decided to take a shower while I perched on the counter, removing my smoky eyes. As I was wiping off the last smudge of mascara, my heart leapt into my throat as a crash filled the apartment, followed by yells.

"What the—"

Kristal leapt out of the shower and, flinging on a bathrobe, raced out of the room after me.

Jake and Ben lay flat on the floor with gags in their mouths, struggling against two tall figures wearing long black leather cloaks. Two more men stood standing near the TV, facing Kristal and I. All four men wore balaclavas that covered everything but their eyes.

But those eyes… they were several shades more vivid than they should have been. And the skin surrounding them was far too pallid to be that of a human.

I was too stunned to even scream, though Kristal managed to. As soon as she opened her mouth, the two men launched forward. One grabbed Kristal, stuffed a gag in her mouth, and wrestled her to the ground, while another blue-eyed man chased after me. I sprinted into the kitchen and grabbed a knife from the drawer as the vampire entered.

The vampire extended his claws.

"You want to play with knives?" he said. "I can play that game."

As he stepped closer, I waved the knife in front of me and backed up against the kitchen counter. Reaching out, I gripped the kettle and, thanking God that there was water left over in it, chucked it over him.

He cried out as the boiling water splashed against his face. It gave me a few seconds to leap over the counter and race back out of the kitchen. I ran for the front door, hoping to make it into the corridor where I could scream for help, but I didn't make it that far. The vampire who had wrestled Kristal to the ground grabbed hold of me and tripped me up.

The blue-eyed vampire reentered the living room, his chest heaving with rage. He gripped my neck and pushed me down to my knees.

"Kristoff," he said, breathing heavily. "Take the Novak boy. I'll take the girl. We may as well bring those two along with us too." He gestured toward Jake and Kristal. "Christian and Sebastian—you bring them. Make sure that none of them scream."

I yelled, but he gagged me. He pushed me flat against the ground, face down, and the next thing I knew, there was a loud thud against my skull and all faded to black.

Chapter 10: Sofia

Derek and I had stayed up with Eli all night, helping him pore over maps in his study. We had made mark upon mark on the maps and taken copious notes, but we'd completely failed to make any sense of the targets.

"I'm just not seeing anything," Eli muttered, rubbing his temples.

"Maybe that's because there is no pattern." I sighed. "We're trying too hard to see something that's not there because it's the only thing we have to cling to right now."

I got up from my chair and paced around the room.

"Mexico... The West Coast," I muttered slowly. "Hm..."

Derek looked up at me.

"I know what you're thinking," he said.

"And it's crazy, right? Nobody here could be doing this."

Derek shook his head.

"I just can't believe any vampire on this island could betray our trust like this on such a massive scale," he said. "I mean, Sofia, we're talking decades! How could any of them pull something like this off for so long? Even leaving aside the inconceivable betrayal, just think about the logistics of it all. Somebody around here would notice."

"It's just that these are all the exact locations The Shade targeted for stealing humans," I said.

Derek rubbed his face in his hands and sighed heavily.

I continued. "And we know that all the vampires who weren't living here when the gates were shut were taken back to Cruor—all those who remained came here."

Eli twirled his pen between his fingers.

"Of course," he said, "it's not like we had any way of verifying that. In theory, there could be other vampires out there that we don't know about."

I turned on Eli and frowned at him.

"But how would they survive? All those other covens were wrecked by the Elders and they deliberately sucked all the vampires they could out of there. And where would they be keeping all these humans? How would they transport themselves there and back?"

Eli shrugged.

"I have no idea," he said. "I'm just saying that we don't have evidence that there aren't other vampires existing on Earth outside of The Shade."

"I don't know," I muttered, stretching my palms out on the table. "Everything points back right here to The Shade. I mean, it's a large island. And we know how hard it is to live exclusively on animal blood. Hell, I find myself craving my own children's blood sometimes."

I locked eyes with Derek. We both shared the same expression. Neither of us wanted to believe that anyone could be betraying our trust and breaking a law of The Shade that we'd instituted two decades ago.

But most of all, neither of us wanted to be the ones to make an accusation like this of our own people.

"Maybe we should investigate," Eli said finally, breaking the silence. "Then we can at least rule it out as an option."

Derek nodded reluctantly.

"All right," he said, clearing his throat. "I guess we'll start once we've had some rest."

"You are aware that our law calls for expulsion if someone here was found guilty?" Eli said, eyeing me.

I nodded, gulping.

Derek and I left Eli and returned to our penthouse. We undressed and got into bed. I snuggled against Derek beneath the sheets.

"Who do you think it could be?" I asked quietly, resting my head against his chest. "I mean, if it was somebody here, who do you think would be behind it?"

Derek shrugged, running his hands along my back.

"I can't answer that. I just know that no matter who is behind this, we can't allow ourselves to go back to our old ways."

Chapter 11: Rose

I woke up to a searing pain in the back of my head. I reached for it and felt a round bump. I was lying on a hard metal floor. I sat up and rubbed my eyes. Ben lay a few feet away from me. I scanned the room for Kristal and Jake, but they were nowhere to be seen.

I was sitting in a dark, damp room. And it felt like we were in some kind of vehicle or vessel, because we were moving forward. The lower deck of a boat, or perhaps the storage chamber of a submarine.

Memories flooding back, I scrambled over to Ben and shook him. He didn't budge at first.

Oh, God.

I turned him over onto his back and placed my ear against his chest. I exhaled sharply when I heard his heartbeat.

"Ben!" I whispered, shaking his shoulders. "Ben, wake up!"

I shook him more violently. When he still didn't open his eyes, I gave him a slap across his face.

That woke him. He groaned and slowly opened his eyes. "Wh-where… what happened?" He sat up, wincing as he rubbed the back of his head.

"I don't know. I just woke up a few seconds ago."

"Where are Kristal and Jake?"

"I told you, I don't know."

He pulled himself off the damp ground and we both sat on the bench.

"I don't understand why these vampires want us," he said. "I thought that vampire left you on the beach, even though he could have easily taken you?"

My brain was throbbing. "Yes," I said. "He let me go. He even seemed scared to come near me."

"Then what the hell are we doing here now? Who are these vampires? Where have they come from? They shouldn't even exist."

I paused and ran a tongue over my parched lips as a more disturbing question entered my mind. *What will they do—or what have they already done—with Kristal and Jake?*

"Some supernatural powers would come in handy now," Ben muttered.

My throat was so dry, I was dying for water. I scanned the room, but there was nothing down here except a few dirty blankets in the corner. I buried my face in my hands and breathed deeply.

If anything happens to them, it will be all our fault.

We should have just gone to that stupid Scottish island.

"Ben," I said suddenly. "Check your pockets. Is your phone still there?"

He reached into his back jeans pockets and shook his head.

"They must have searched us and confiscated it."

I swore.

Ben got up and walked over to the metal door of the chamber and banged his fists against it.

"We're awake, you assholes!" he yelled, his voice as hoarse as my own. "Some water would be appreciated."

Ben returned to his seat. Several minutes later, footsteps sounded outside and the door creaked open.

A tall ginger vampire stepped in and placed a tin bowl filled with water down on the floor. I recognized those light blue eyes of his instantly.

"What have you done with them?" I hissed, jumping up and running toward the door.

He slammed it shut before I could reach it.

I shouted in frustration and kicked the door. I looked down at the bowl and brought it over to the bench.

"You have some first," Ben said.

I took a sip, then passed the bowl to him. We alternated until we'd drunk it all up. It tasted stale and metallic, like it had been stored in some kind of old rusting container for too long, but at least it wasn't sea water.

Ben placed the bowl on the floor and I rested my head against his shoulder. He wrapped his arms around me and pulled me closer against him.

"I miss our parents," Ben admitted.

"Me too."

Chapter 12: Sofia

Under the questioning glares of all the vampires on the island, we made them all gather in the large clearing outside the Black Heights and wait in line as we called them into the mountain chambers for interviewing. Claudia, Ashley and Zinnia produced a particularly loud symphony of complaining, so we saw those three early. Eli, Derek and I each interviewed a vampire at a time, but it still took all day even though each interview didn't last long.

We even interviewed those closest to us: Vivienne, Xavier and my own father, Aiden. Although there was no chance in hell they'd betray us, we had to do it.

Lastly, we asked ourselves the same questions and

concluded that each of us had alibis.

As it turned out, every single vampire on the island had alibis for the night the Cancún kidnappings took place... except for Aiden and Abby.

Eli, Derek and I sat alone in one of the mountain chambers we now used for storing sacks of food for the human inhabitants of the island.

"Well, leaving aside my father and Abby for a moment, everyone else seems to be innocent," I said. "Of course, unless this is a mass operation with multiple vampires going behind our backs and providing each other with alibis."

"I suppose that it's possible," Derek said. "But that would be hard to orchestrate on such short notice. We asked detailed information and it would have been hard to not slip up."

"So, we're left with Aiden and Abby," Eli said, frowning at the long list of names of vampires in front of us.

"Ludicrous," I said. "Neither of them would do something like this."

"So, since you're convinced of that, we can cross everyone at The Shade off of our list of possible suspects," Eli said, dropping the list on the table and leaning back in his chair, stretching out his legs.

I nodded.

"So we're back to square one," Derek muttered.

"I'm going to turn in now," Eli said, standing up. "I'll think more about all of this when I'm fresh in the morning."

Derek and I returned to our own penthouse. We both sat at the dining table and sipped on some blood before heading off to bed. As we were both drifting off, a pounding on our front door sent us shooting up out of bed.

Derek swung the door open to see Eli standing at the door, covered in sweat, eyes alight with panic.

"I just tuned into the news before sleeping," Eli said, panting. "There have been more kidnappings. Hawaii."

He came rushing in.

"There were two incidents… some days apart from each other. The second incident," he said, gasping for breath. "R-Rose and Benjamin Novak, both twenty-one years old. Staying with Kristal and Jake Palmer, eighteen and nineteen. They said on the radio. All four are missing."

"What? But they're not anywhere near Hawaii," I breathed. "They're in Scotland. And they're seventeen. It must just be a coincidence."

"Twins! They're twins!"

Whatever blood I still had in my pale face drained out of me. I looked up at Derek. His jaw dropped open, eyes widening.

"Come! I'll show you," Eli urged. "They showed photos. I saw them. They're your twins, goddamn it!"

Chapter 13: Rose

I must have drifted off in Ben's arms, because I woke to the sensation of the submarine shuddering so violently both Ben and I were thrown to the ground. I groaned as my head connected with the wall. Then my stomach lurched—it felt as if we were surfacing.

Several minutes passed in silence, but then there were shouts and banging overhead. It sounded like a violent argument was going on.

"Do you realize who their father is?"

"Obviously. That's why we took them."

"Stellan, you're a bloody fool."

"For carrying out Annora's orders?"

"Liar. Even she wouldn't order something like this."

"She did. As soon as you told her you'd almost taken the girl."

"Liar!"

More crashing. Shouts. Screams. Then heavy footsteps descended the steps outside the door. Wood splintered and metal bent as someone kicked the door down in three violent motions.

A tall young man stood over us, a deep gash across his cheek, his face covered with dirt and sweat. His shirt was ripped, revealing his muscled chest beneath.

The vampire I'd danced with on the beach.

Caleb.

His deep brown eyes settled on us.

"Hurry," he said, his chest heaving. "I need to get you out of here."

Ben and I shot to our feet. Caleb gripped my arm and pushed me up the stairs in front of him, while Ben followed closely behind.

As I was about to step up onto the upper deck, Caleb jerked me back.

"Wait," he whispered.

He climbed up on the same step where I was standing, his rock-hard chest pressing against me as he strained his neck to see what was happening on the deck above.

"Now!"

He almost lifted me off my feet as he pulled me up with him. I glanced back anxiously to check that Ben was still following us.

The deck was in chaos. The submarine was split into a large control room at the front, and then an area with more seats at the back. Vampires clawed and ripped at each other.

I didn't have much time to look around though, because soon Caleb was pushing me up a narrow ladder. We reached yet another level of more vampires fighting. He ran with us across the floor until we reached another ladder. Again he pushed me up and this time, there was an open hatch up ahead. Rain poured onto my face. Caleb gripped my thighs and pushed me up. I held onto the metal edge of the hatch and pulled myself the rest of the way.

It was night and we appeared to be floating in the middle of the ocean. Another black submarine floated parallel to us. I scrambled further along the roof of the submarine. The heavy rain was impairing my vision, and the already smooth surface became even more precarious. My foot slipped. I screamed as I slid down the side of the submarine, trying to find anything to grip onto, but there was nothing. I closed my eyes, bracing myself to fall face forward into the ocean, when a strong hand wrapped around my ankle.

The hand pulled up until I was once again on the flat

surface of the roof. When I sat up, I found myself looking into Caleb's intense eyes.

"Careful!" he scolded.

My hair stood on end as I looked down at the rough, dark waters I'd almost slid into.

I looked around me and breathed out in relief to see Ben climbing out of the hatch. He lowered himself down and crouched down next to me on the roof, pulling me closer to him.

Caleb whistled, and vampires began also retreating out of the hatch, filling up the remaining space of the roof. The last one out slammed the hatch shut behind him and about four vampires pushed down on it as vampires within the vessel tried to break out.

Caleb whistled again, and the submarine floating next to us neared. As soon as it was within jumping distance, the vampires on the roof began to leap onto it. Now all of them had crossed but one who remained applying pressure to the hatch so that the vampires within it couldn't get out.

Ben pushed me forward toward Caleb.

"Hurry, take my sister," Ben said, eyeing the hatch.

Caleb nodded and stared down at me.

"Climb onto my back. You *must* grip tight."

Trembling, I locked my arms around his neck and wrapped my legs around his waist. I closed my eyes as he took the leap. We landed with a thud on the roof of the other submarine and Caleb had to grip a pipe to prevent us from skidding off.

"Now, into the hatch," he ordered.

"No! Wait!" I gasped, fighting against his attempts to push me into the submarine.

The last vampire who was holding down the hatch on the other sub lost his footing and slipped into the ocean.

That left Ben all by himself.

"Ben!" I screamed. "Jump!"

He leapt, but the ginger vampire who had just climbed out of the hatch jumped with him at the same time and pulled him down into the ocean.

"No! Ben!"

The vampire caught hold of my struggling brother and pulled him back up onto his sub.

"Caleb! Do something!" I screamed as the vampire wrestled Ben back through the hatch. I fought against Caleb's strong grip, trying to break free.

But then it was too late for even Caleb to leap back over. The hatch slammed shut and the submarine lowered itself into the depths of the dark ocean.

Chapter 14: Sofia

I stared at Eli's TV, barely believing what I was seeing.

Passport photos of my twins flashed before the screen.

"Those are the suspects." Eli pointed to the screen as CCTV footage showed two tall men dressed in long black cloaks, wearing gloves and black hats, entering the apartment foyer.

Derek stood up and swore as the two men entered the elevator after Rose and presumably her friend Kristal. "But how did any of this happen? How the hell did they get to Hawaii?"

"Oh, God," I said. "You know how much they were complaining about going to Scotland. They must have figured out a way to get to Hawaii instead."

Derek slammed his fists down against the table. "And who are they?" He looked like he wanted to climb into the TV and rip the two men to shreds there and then. It was impossible to tell who they were. For all we knew, they could have been regular humans looking to prey on two innocent girls.

"There's footage of the two of them entering," Eli said, his hands shaking as he held the remote, "followed by two more a few minutes later—see?—but there's no footage of them ever exiting. That's what's got the police so confused. They have no idea how they could have gotten all four of those teens out of there without being caught on camera. The last footage they have is the four men entering the apartment. After that, nothing."

"We need to get out of here," I said, standing up. "We have to find them."

Derek and I stormed out of Eli's penthouse and raced through the woods to the Sanctuary. Derek ripped the heavy wooden door from its hinges with his bare hands as we raced through the corridors to their bedroom.

"Ibrahim! Corrine!" we shouted as we burst in.

The married couple sat up in bed, looking at both of us groggily and rubbing their eyes.

"Sofia?" Corrine mumbled. "Derek? What is this?"

"The twins," I shrieked. "They've been kidnapped."

That woke her up faster than a bucket of ice water.

"We need you to take us to Honolulu, Hawaii this instant."

She and Ibrahim stumbled out of bed, wrapping robes around their bare forms. Corrine gripped my shoulders, shaking me. "What? What are you saying? Hawaii?"

"There's no time for explanation now."

Corrine swore, clasping a hand to her mouth. "This is all my fault."

"What?" Derek gripped Corrine's shoulders. "What are you saying?"

"For the twins' birthday, Rose asked me to change the dates on her and Ben's passports. She promised that it was just to allow them to—"

"Derek, there's no time for talk," I urged. "Take us there. Now! Hurry!"

Ibrahim and Corrine held onto us and a few seconds later, we had vanished from The Shade in a whirl of colors.

Chapter 15: Rose

I screamed as the shadow of the submarine disappeared completely beneath the water.

Caleb tightened his grip around my waist and pulled me up toward the hatch, but I continued to struggle.

"Let me go!" I cried.

He gripped both of my wrists with one hand and lowered me into the hatch with the other. Hands beneath me grabbed my legs and pulled me down. When my feet touched the ground and Caleb slammed the hatch shut, my knees gave way and I crumpled to the floor, sobbing.

"Ben! Ben! No!"

I shut my eyes tight, and prayed that when I opened

them, I'd wake up back in Kristal's condo. This would all be a dreadful nightmare. I'd get up and rush into Ben's bedroom to find him snoring and splayed out on the mattress in his blue pajamas.

"Ben, Ben, Ben," I breathed, as if saying his name would bring him back to me.

Caleb crouched down beside me. I looked up into his brown eyes, my own eyes blurred with tears.

"I'll get your brother back," he said, his voice deep, his face ashen, dark hair soaking wet from the rain.

He stood up and began walking away.

"Wait," I stammered, scrambling to my feet and following after him. "How? How will you get Ben back?"

Caleb didn't look back at me as he continued walking along the narrow corridor of the submarine, injured vampires zigging and zagging in and out of rooms and crossing over our path as we walked.

He didn't answer me until he reached a door at the bow of the vessel, pushed it open and took a seat in the control room, behind hundreds of buttons and dials, next to a vampire whom I assumed was the captain of the submarine.

Once seated, Caleb swiveled in his seat and faced me again.

"I'm going to speak to his superior. He had no authorization to do what he has done."

I sat down in one of the spare seats behind them as the vampire on the right moved the vessel forward.

"But where are we going? Why don't we chase after their submarine and get Ben back right this instant? Just like you rescued me."

Caleb shook his head and set his eyes forward through the window screen.

"It's too late for that now."

"But what if they do something to him in the meantime?"

"They won't harm him."

"How do you know?"

"I know."

Racing forward in the opposite direction from my kidnapped brother was the most painful experience I remembered having. "Where are we going now?" I breathed, tears spilling from my eyes again.

"Back to base."

"Base?"

"You'll see," Caleb said, impatience beginning to show in his voice. "Enough questions."

I gripped the back of his seat and, wiping away my tears with the back of my sleeve, looked forward through the screen to try to make sense of where we were headed. All I could see was an endless expanse of black ocean.

I sat back in my seat and closed my eyes.

Please, Ben. Be safe. Please.

Then I thought about the mobile phone they had confiscated. Our parents were used to us calling thrice a week. Usually Mondays, Wednesdays and Fridays. If we didn't call them, they'd get suspicious.

But how on earth will they find us? They'll contact the adventure company's office only to find that we checked out long ago.

Goddamn it. We should have called to tell them about those vampires.

Tears threatened to consume me again, even though there was no point to them. Tears weren't going to help bring Ben back. Or help our parents find us. I looked up at Caleb.

He's our only hope.

I still didn't understand his motivation for helping us, and I couldn't trust him. But he was the only glimmer of light we had in this darkness.

I sneezed. My clothes were soaking from the rain.

Caleb turned around in his chair to look at me and immediately got up. "Come with me."

I followed him out of the control room, along the passageway. We stopped outside a door. He knocked three times.

"Frieda," he called.

The door opened and a tall ebony-skinned vampire

nursing a painful-looking gash in her arm appeared in the doorway.

"Do you have anything this girl could change into?"

Her chestnut-brown eyes settled on me and she nodded.

"Yes, I'm sure I can fix her up with something. Come in."

Celeb placed his hand on the small of my back and nudged me inside. Frieda closed the door behind me.

"Let's see what we've got here," she said.

The cabin was tiny—barely large enough for a single bed and a cabinet. She crouched down and pulled open a drawer in the chest in the corner.

The first thing she pulled out was a towel. Then a long cotton nightdress.

"It's not much, but it's better than staying in those wet clothes."

She placed both on her bed and left the room for me to change.

I wasn't sure what to do with my sopping wet pajamas so I just put them in a corner of the room. I dried myself as much as I could with the towel, then pulled the nightdress over my head. I wrapped up my wet hair in the towel to form a turban.

I opened the door to find Frieda waiting outside.

"Thank you," I murmured.

She nodded and was about to shut herself back in the

room when I asked, "Could I ask you a few questions?"

"I think it's best you ask Caleb any questions you have. I don't know how much you're allowed to know."

She shut the door and I made my way back to the control room. When I pushed open the door, Caleb turned around and looked me over briefly, then turned back to face the glass screen.

I sat down in my seat.

"How much longer until we arrive at your 'base'?" I asked.

"About three hours."

Chapter 16: Rose

The submarine slowed to a halt and rose to the surface.

"We're here," Caleb said.

He stood up and I followed him out of the control room, along the narrow passageway, until we reached the ladder leading to the hatch.

He climbed up first, and I followed next, the rest of the vampires lining up behind me.

"Oh," I breathed as soon as I looked around outside.

The sudden cold was the first thing that hit me—it felt like we were in the Arctic. Everything seemed to be covered in snow. We had stopped outside a small port. Behind us in the far distance the rays of the sun beat down against the water, but here they were blocked out due to the same protective charm that The Shade had.

I turned to look in front of me. Caleb had climbed down onto the icy wooden jetty and was looking up at me, hands crossed over his chest.

Shivering, I climbed down after him, almost slipping on Frieda's long night gown in the process.

When I cast a cursory look around the island, leaving aside that it was covered with snow, it did appear similar to The Shade. There were thick woods—although the trees weren't nearly as tall here—and I spotted a mountain range in the distance.

"Where do you vampires come from?"

Caleb remained silent, his eyes set forward.

When I repeated my question, he stared at me and said, "The less you know, the safer you'll be. My priority is to get you and your brother back to your parents. I'll tell you everything you need to know. Anything else you may ask is irrelevant and I suggest you keep it to yourself."

I wanted to argue back, but the seriousness in his expression chilled me more than the weather.

Once we had crossed the beach, I looked back to get a better look at the vampires who were a part of this coven. I spotted among them some of the men I'd seen that first night I'd met Caleb at the beach party. There were perhaps fifty vampires in total—a mixture of men and women. All of them appeared to be young vampires, around the age of twenty.

Leaving the beach, we veered left toward the foothills of the mountains. And then I saw it looming in the distance. A giant grey stone-walled castle, with half a dozen sharp black-roofed turrets, built up among some of the highest peaks. Just looking at how high up it was made my head dizzy and my knees weak.

Caleb looked down at me.

"It's a long way up. I'll have to carry you."

He didn't wait for my permission. Placing one arm behind my knees and wrapping the other around my waist, he picked me up. Then he began racing up the narrow winding steps leading toward the castle. His speed left me breathless, the cruel wind whipping past my ears. I wrapped my arms around his neck and looked over his shoulder at the other vampires running behind us.

By the time we arrived at the top, about ten minutes later, my whole body was shivering uncontrollably. Caleb looked like he'd just taken a casual stroll in the park, not sprinted up a colossal ice-covered mountain.

He set me down on the ground once we reached the heavy oak doors leading into the castle. He pushed them both open. They swung backward, creaking.

Cautiously, I stepped in after him. We stepped into a giant hall, lit only by burning candles in the corners of the room, their flames licking the shadowy walls. Walking across the black marble floors, we made our way toward a grand staircase.

The place was so spooky I instinctively reached out and gripped Caleb's hand. He didn't look down at me, but his arm tensed. Then his hand closed ever so slightly around mine.

We climbed up to the first level—leaving all the vampires behind us to go their separate ways—and continued up winding staircase after winding staircase until we reached what appeared to be the top of one of the turrets.

We stopped outside a black door, engraved with some weird-looking language. Caleb let go of my hand and knocked.

"Annora!" he called. "Open up. It's Caleb."

The door swung open to reveal a tall, pale black-haired woman with cool grey eyes.

"And what have we here?" she said, looking down at me coldly.

Caleb gripped my arm and pulled me inside.

The room was rectangular, with an oblong table at one end and several silk-covered chaise longues at the other. The velvet curtains had been drawn.

"This," Caleb began as he shut the door behind us, "is the Novak girl. Stellan kidnapped her and her brother."

Stellan. That must be the ginger-haired bastard's name.

"So what are you doing with this girl?" Annora said. "I instructed Stellan to bring both twins to his island. I never wanted them here."

"You what?" Caleb's jaw dropped as he stared at the young woman.

She smiled coldly and walked up to him, running a finger across his cheek. He flinched at her touch, but he didn't back away.

"Yes, Caleb. I told Stellan to kidnap them."

"Are you insane? Why would you do that?" Caleb fumed. "Our task is difficult enough as it is without—"

"When you told me you'd almost taken this Novak girl that night you went to the beach, it got me thinking…" She looked down at me, wrinkling her nose. "But now's not the time."

"Christ." Caleb exhaled, lifting a hand to his forehead.

Annora looked him over sternly. "Did you try to ambush Stellan?"

Caleb nodded. "I didn't think you'd give such an order."

She chuckled and wrapped an arm around Caleb's waist, while the other hand lifted his chin up to face her. Again, he flinched at her advances, but didn't step away.

"Do you still have no faith in me, after all this time?"

He scowled. "Whatever your plan is," he said through gritted teeth, "keeping these twins as prisoners is going to cause more mess than it's worth. We need to return them both immediately."

"No," she said, the smile on her lips fading. "The Novak boy will remain with Stellan. And since you've brought the girl here, she may as well remain here under your rule. Come to think of it, it's probably better that the two aren't kept together."

Caleb's jaw twitched. "And what am I to do with her?"

"For now, you can treat her as a guest. Give her her own room. Of course, you'll need to inform her of what will happen should she try to escape."

"Wait, no. Please." I stepped forward and got down on my knees in front of her. "Please, let us go."

Caleb gripped my arm and pulled me away from her.

"Please!" I shouted, as he dragged me out of the room. "I need to see my brother! At least bring him here, or allow me to go there!"

Caleb slammed the door shut behind us. Once we were outside, he swore and smashed his fists against the stone wall.

I held my breath as I stared at him, tears welling in my eyes again.

"What's going to happen to my brother?"

"Never try to plead with that witch," he said, inhaling deeply as though trying to reel in his temper. "It will only make her more bent on her course of action."

"She's a witch?"

He nodded, grimacing.

"But you're the ruler of this place? Just take us back home! Why do you have to listen to that bitch?"

He caught my hand and pulled me down the stairs with him. "For your sake, I hope she didn't hear you call her that."

"Answer my question," I said, tugging on his hand as I struggled to keep up with his speed.

He ignored me and continued to drag me down the steps.

I stopped in my tracks, refusing to take another step. Letting go of my hand, he gripped my midriff and flung me over his shoulder.

"Put me down!" I gasped, winded.

When he finally put me down, we were standing outside an open door. He led me through to a bedroom. It was cold, just like the rest of the castle, although the room was comfortable—luxurious even—with its velvet curtains and thick duvets.

The vampire turned to leave.

"No! You can't just walk out on me like this," I yelled, running after him. "I need answers!"

He slammed the door shut, and the key twisted in the lock.

Chapter 17: Rose

After about an hour of screaming and bashing the front door, it was clear that nobody was going to let me out. My fists raw from pounding against the rough wood, I walked back into the bedroom and drew open the balcony doors. I stepped outside onto the balcony and looked around.

That witch never said anything about locking me in here. I'm supposed to be a guest.

First I looked out toward the sea—it appeared to be night now, since the sun no longer glistened against the waves outside of the boundary.

I shuddered. Below me was a steep drop of hundreds of feet, down onto jagged mountain cliffs. I was on one of the highest floors of the building. It would be suicide to escape this way. There was nothing to hold on to. Just rock.

There were rows of balconies, both on my level and also the level above. But the balconies were too far apart for me to jump safely from one to the other.

I left the balcony and looked around the bedroom. I headed straight for the closet and was relieved to see a warm, thick robe. I wrapped it around myself and felt a little warmer, though still frozen to the bone.

There didn't appear to be central heating in this castle. Although there was an old-fashioned fireplace in the corner of my room. It was filled with dry logs and some coal. Grabbing a set of matches on the mantelpiece, I lit the fire until it was stoked enough to warm the room. I lay in bed and huddled beneath the blankets, finally feeling my body return to a healthy temperature.

That was when the door unlatched. I rushed out of the bedroom in time to see the door slam shut and the key turn again. On the floor was a tray. There was a jug of water, an empty metal cup, and a metal bowl. I bent down closer to sniff the bowl. Oatmeal.

Oatmeal, huh. If this is what you feed your guests, I hate to think what you feed your prisoners.

I drank the water, but I didn't have any appetite for food. Especially not oatmeal.

I shuddered as I wondered if Ben was being treated any better. Somehow, under Stellan's rule, I doubted it.

Once I'd finished drinking the water, I curled back in bed beneath the covers and tried to fall asleep. But I couldn't. I lay for hours, staring at the chandelier hanging from the ceiling. I couldn't get the harrowing images of Ben being sucked back into that black submarine out my mind. I couldn't stop thinking about how worried our parents would be once they found out we weren't in Scotland.

It must have been well past midnight when a thump reverberated across my ceiling. Then another thump. It sounded like it was coming from the room directly above mine. The thumps got louder and more violent until the chandelier was swinging in its place.

What in the world?

"Stop," a man shouted, making my heart leap into my throat.

Glass smashed. Then more shouts.

I got out of bed and walked out onto the balcony, shivering as I drew the robe closer around me.

"Don't make me do this."

The voice was clearer this time. *The balcony door upstairs must be open.*

Then a female, shrill and breathless: "Why do you make this so difficult?"

More crashing and thumping on the floor.

"Caleb!"

Caleb?

Wood snapped.

"You bitch."

Another thud against my floor and then a groan of pain.

"I think we're done for this evening," the female voice said.

Her voice was clearer that time, as though she was standing right by the balcony. Clear enough to realize who was up there with him: the witch.

I crouched down and listened with bated breath as footsteps disappeared. A door slammed shut in the distance. Then footsteps sounded again on the balcony above. I ducked down closer into the shadows as two hands gripped the banister above. I heard heavy breathing.

I stayed in my spot, even though my bare feet were beginning to freeze, until he left the balcony and the doors closed behind him. I did the same with my doors and climbed back into bed.

I tried to close my eyes and finally fall asleep now that the noises had stopped, but now I felt more awake than ever. I couldn't get the sounds of the violence going on up there out of my head. Even though they had stopped, they continued to echo around in my mind—most of all, the way Caleb had groaned out in pain.

What was that witch doing to him?

Chapter 18: Rose

I ended up climbing out of bed in the early hours of the morning and, placing my blanket and pillows near the front door, lay there. I obviously wasn't going to get a wink of sleep that night, so I figured that I might as well wait by the door in case someone came to give me breakfast in the morning. I needed to catch whoever it was.

I was right in my presumption. At about nine o'clock according to the old clock in my corridor, the door creaked open. I scrambled to my feet and stuck my foot in the gap, wedging it open. Gripping the door, I pried it open further.

Standing in the doorway was Frieda, another tray of what appeared to be more gruel and a jug of water in her hands.

She almost dropped the tray from the surprise of seeing me.

I had to think fast. "Frieda," I said, "I really can't stand oatmeal. In fact, I'm allergic to oats. I didn't eat the portion you gave me yesterday. Can I please have something else?"

She stared at me, as though not sure what to make of me.

"That's just the standard fare we feed all humans here. Afraid we don't have much else."

"Can you please take me to the kitchens? I'm sure there must be something better…"

"Listen, I'm no cook. I'm just bringing you this up because Caleb specifically asked me to—I don't know why he requested me."

"Okay, well, just tell me which direction the kitchens are in and I'll find it myself."

She frowned at me. "Caleb didn't tell me that you could be wandering about by yourself."

"Well, your witch said I'm a guest here. Not a prisoner."

When she continued to look hesitant, I said, "Look, I promise you that I'll be back within half an hour. I've been locked up in this little room for ages. I need to stretch my legs."

"All right," she said, sighing. "But I'll come with you. I'm sure Caleb wouldn't object if I accompanied you."

She put the tray down on the ground inside my apartment, then caught hold of my hand and led me away down the dark corridor.

As we descended down to the lower levels of the castle, I didn't notice many other vampires roaming about. Perhaps because it was still early. "So do you steal away humans regularly then?" I asked, trying to sound casual, but failing miserably.

She stopped in her tracks and eyed me, as if wondering whether or not she should answer.

"Hm," she said. "We go once every few months. It's getting harder and harder."

"What do you mean?"

She frowned at me again.

"Well, obviously after years of disappearances, we can only go to open areas where there aren't CCTV cameras, or we'll get caught on film. It will be much more difficult if our faces are publicized everywhere."

Years of disappearances.

Why am I so ignorant of all this? Why didn't our parents tell us?

"And all those humans you catch, you just use them for blood?"

"That's not your business."

"Okay," I said quickly. "Well, can you tell me where all of you vampires came from? Because I've lived in The Shade all my life and I never knew there were any other covens left."

"One thing you'd best learn sooner rather than later is that the less you know, the better."

I refrained from asking more questions as we arrived in the kitchens—a chamber underground. There were shelves filled with bottles containing a red liquid that made me shudder. There were also bottles of liquor.

As it turned out, Frieda was right about not having much more than oatmeal. There were several sacks of oats in the corner of the room, and the only other thing I spotted was a bowl of apples and bananas. I grabbed two apples and a banana. If I had to eat oatmeal, at least these would make it a little more bearable.

We walked back up the staircases until we arrived again outside my room. She opened the door for me to step inside. Just as she was about to close the door, I held out my hand to stop her.

"What goes on up there at night?" I asked, pointing toward the ceiling.

Frieda glared at me.

"What goes on up there is between him and the witch, understood?"

With that, she stormed off.

Chapter 19: Rose

She forgot to lock the door.

I must have agitated her so much that she'd just walked off with the key still in her pocket. Dropping the fruit, I eased the door open and looked either way along the dark corridor. Seeing nobody there, I stepped out, careful to shut the door again behind me.

Barefoot, I made my way back toward the staircase I'd just come up with with Frieda. I crouched down by the banister and looked down to see if anybody was on the stairs below. Satisfied that there was nobody, I began my descent to the ground floor. My breath rasping, my heart hammering against my chest, I managed to make it to the bottom floor without anybody noticing. It appeared to be empty. I ran straight to the oak doors and tried to turn the heavy metal door handle. It wouldn't budge, no matter how much I twisted it.

Damn it.

Windows.

I left the front door and moved to my right, into the first room that was open. It appeared to be some sort of dining hall, with high towering ceilings, stained-glass windows and a long oak table in the center.

I threw myself beneath the table and crawled beneath it until I reached one of the windows. I grasped the handle and it pushed open easily. But again, I found myself staring down at a steep drop, hardly any less steep than outside my balcony. There was nothing to hold onto, no way to climb down.

There's no way I'll survive that. Even if I did by some miracle survive the drop, I'd freeze in the snow before I could even reach the woods.

The only escape seemed to be out the front door.

I made my way to the staircase and began climbing back up. I passed a couple of male vampires on my way up, but thankfully they didn't pay much notice to me. They must have assumed that I had permission to walk around.

Instead of returning to my room, I climbed up one more

flight of stairs until I reached Caleb's floor. I inched toward his door and placed my ear against it. I couldn't hear anything.

I gripped the handle and tried to open it, but it was locked. I knocked.

I heard a low groan and footsteps walking toward the door. The door unlatched to reveal a half-naked, bleary-eyed Caleb. His dark hair was ruffled and he wore a sheet wrapped low round his waist. My breath hitched at his bare torso.

"You... How did you—"

Before he could say another word, I pushed the door open wider and slipped inside.

"If you *accidentally* leave that main door open," I said, forcing my eyes up to his face, "I'll escape and the witch will never know."

He walked into what was presumably his bedroom and returned wearing a black robe. "Who let you out?"

When I ignored his question, he reached to open the door but I slammed my back against it.

"I'm not going anywhere until you give me some answers."

He rubbed his face with his hands and sighed heavily. "I don't need this hassle. Get out."

"Open the main door, and I'll disappear into the night. Nobody will ever know you let me escape. It could have been anyone in this castle who left the door open."

He shook his head and glared at me.

"You really think it's that easy for a human to escape this place? There's a spell around this island to keep it cold. Even if you made it down to the sea without getting caught or dying of hypothermia, and somehow broke into one of the submarines and figured out how to navigate it, there's another spell preventing anyone getting out unless they have permission."

"Then why don't you just leave with me now?" I said, tugging on the sleeve of his robe. "Or when the witch is doing something else. She never has to know."

It seemed that he'd had enough of the conversation. He marched me outside and dragged me down the stairs.

He stopped outside of my door and pushed it open.

"No!"

I clung onto the doorframe as he tried to bundle me inside.

"You're not locking me up in here again."

He grabbed both of my hands and pried them away from the door. I leaped at him, wrapping my arms around his shoulders and my legs around his waist. My sudden motion made him lose his footing and he stumbled backward into the hallway, his back slamming against the wall.

He gripped my legs and pried them away from him. Then

he did the same with my arms.

I stood in the hallway, glaring at him. He glared back at me.

"All right!" he shouted. "I won't lock the door. But if you attempt to escape, you'll end up getting yourself killed or worse. Don't say that I didn't warn you."

I didn't nod, but I didn't object either. He turned on his heel to leave. I was tempted to shout out after him why he couldn't just escape with me and why he had to listen to what the witch said, but I figured that this was a good first step. I was no longer locked up in that little apartment like a prisoner.

Instead, I was locked up in the castle.

I can't believe he couldn't smuggle me out of this place if he really wanted to.

Chapter 20: Rose

That evening as I was lying in bed, I heard the sounds again.

Thump. Thump. Thump. Against my ceiling. I threw the covers off me and stood up on my bed, trying to get closer to the noises.

"Say it," the witch hissed.

I heard another groan. And the sound of a fireplace spitting.

"I'm losing patience with you."

The smashing of glass. The screeching of heavy furniture against the floor.

Grabbing my dressing gown, I ran out my front door and crept up the stairs. I didn't stop until I reached Caleb's door.

I pressed my ear against it, the voices now clearer.

"I need you to say it."

"No," Caleb grunted, low and deep. "Never."

I pushed the door open, wincing as it clicked. I froze.

Oh, no.

There was a silence as the witch came into view at the other end of the corridor. She wore a long dark green dress, her loose hair running down her back. She sported a black eye and a deep bloody cut beneath her collarbone.

As soon as our eyes locked, fury sparked in hers. She walked over to me.

"Well, look who's here," she whispered, her voice dangerously low.

Before I could stagger back, she reached out and clutched my throat. I tried to scream, but it came out as a garbled choke. She was crushing my windpipe.

"Didn't your mother ever teach you that it's rude to eavesdrop?"

I gripped her hand, trying to pry her clammy fingers away from my throat, but it was useless.

"Leave her."

The words came as a deep growl from across the corridor. Caleb stood in the doorway, a gash beneath his lower eye, his shirt ripped and blood seeping through from several gashes on his chest.

The witch chuckled and continued to grip my throat, applying more pressure by the second.

Caleb launched himself at the witch. Gripping her neck, he held her in a choke until she released me.

I slid down the wall, gasping and rubbing my throat.

"Don't take this out on her," he snarled, hurling the witch against the marble floor. "And don't drag her into your sick game."

"You dare," the witch hissed, her eyes dilating with fury, her cheeks crimson.

"Yes, I dare," Caleb bellowed back down at her. "There's nothing more of me you can break."

The witch got to her feet, straightened out her dress, then after glaring daggers at me she stormed out of the room, slamming the door behind her.

His eyes burning with fury and his whole body still heaving, Caleb turned around and walked further into his apartment. He disappeared into a room at the end of the corridor, but he didn't shut his door. I got to my feet and approached the door. I pushed the door open and entered.

As I looked around, I was horrified by the state the place was in. His spacious apartment appeared to be open plan—his bedroom, kitchen and lounge all ran into each other. The wallpaper was torn, canvas paintings on the wall ripped. Bloodstained bedding was strewn all over the floor. The curtains were ripped almost to shreds. Caleb sat in the corner of the bedroom, his back turned to me, in a wooden armchair. A bottle of liquor by his side, he was pouring himself a shot. I watched as he downed it in one gulp.

I approached his chair tentatively.

"You shouldn't be here," he said, without turning around. But he made no motion to pick me up and throw me out the door as he had done the day before.

I walked around and stood so that I was facing him. I stared at the gash beneath his right eye that was beginning to heal slowly.

"What happened?" I breathed.

He shook his head and downed another shot.

"Why do you allow her to treat you this way? Are you ruler of this island or not?"

He got up and walked over to the open balcony door, where he stood, gazing out at the starry night sky. The full moon shone down on his chiseled form.

The living room and kitchen area were in a much less damaged state than the bedroom. My eyes fell upon a collection of classical instruments in the corner of the lounge.

Since he didn't seem to be willing to answer my questions, I asked, "You play?"

He looked over his shoulder at me as I pointed toward the instruments in the corner.

A faint smile crossed his face.

"No," he said quietly. "Not any more."

I walked over to the instruments and was impressed by the quality of their build. They were covered in a thick coat of dust, as though they hadn't been touched for months, maybe even years. Although I specialized in the piano and the harp, I could play most instruments I saw here. My father was a master of many and had given Ben and I lessons in most.

I absentmindedly ran my hand over the top of the grand piano. Lifting up its cover, I sat down and stretched out my fingers over the keys. I began to play a tune. Soft, haunting, melancholic. I smiled bitterly—my father had played this for my mother when they'd first met.

Caleb left the balcony and walked over to me, placing his glass on top of the piano, staring down at me as I played. It was unnerving at first, playing beneath the intensity of his gaze, but I didn't let it distract me.

When I finished, I looked up at him. He hadn't moved an inch the whole time. His eyes had glazed over, as if his mind had wandered somewhere else.

"I'd like you to play for me again… Rose," he whispered finally.

The way he said my name was gentle, as though his tongue was caressing the word. The attention he was giving me was unnerving—I was used to him brushing me away whenever he could. *Perhaps it's just because he's drunk? I sure do strange things when I'm drunk.* I stared into his eyes, trying to read him. The way he was looking at me was confusing. It was as though he was conflicted as to whether he ought to be looking at me at all.

"O-okay," I murmured.

Although I didn't get any of the answers that I needed that night, one thing had become clearer than ever. If anyone had the power and ability to get me out of there and save my brother, it was Caleb. And at that moment, befriending him—or at least trying to—seemed to be the only available option.

Chapter 21: Rose

I was woken the next morning by a knock at my door. I got out of bed and looked around. But whoever it was had already vanished.

A black bundle sat on my doorstep. I picked it up and shut the door, then walked over to my bed and unravelled it.

Wrapped up in a black sheet were clothes. Underwear, beautiful gowns, fluffy slippers, and a warm woolen coat.

About time, I thought. *I've been walking around in this apartment barefoot with blankets pulled over me in this smelly old nightgown ever since I got here.*

I took a shower and, discarding the old nightgown in a bin, I pulled on fresh underwear. I was relieved that it was the stretchy, comfortable type and not the itchy, lacy kind. Then I reached for one of the gowns and pulled it over my head. It was deep purple and made of silk. I layered the coat on top and looked in the mirror.

Hm. Not too shabby.

I brushed my hands through my hair to tame it.

Now all I need is Kristal's makeup.

Kristal. Her name sent a dagger through my chest. I prayed that nothing had happened to her or her brother. *If anything does, it will be all Ben's and my fault.*

I have to get out of here and save all of them.

Putting on the slippers, I decided to leave the room and go for another roam around the castle.

Walking around confirmed that Caleb was my only hope. Apart from Frieda, no other vampire would even speak to me. They avoided me in the corridors. I tried to talk to one of them, and she gave me a funny look and hurried off.

I reached the ground floor and walked from hall to hall until, at the back of the building, I found the entrance to the kitchen Frieda had taken me to.

I walked around, running my hand along the metal counter. The kitchen was huge—as big as any of the other halls.

I wonder where they keep all the humans? If these vampires drink their blood, it would be convenient to keep them near the kitchen. Perhaps in a dungeon. That's normally where the poor mortals end up being stuffed in fairy tales.

I looked around the room for any sign of a door in the wall, or a trap door, but found none.

Hmm.

And then I heard it. Distant sobbing. I held my breath as I tried to make out from which direction it was coming.

I retraced my steps back out of the kitchen and took a sharp right turn. I walked along the corridor until I reached an open door. I peeped through it. In a hall I'd never passed by before, a woman perched on the windowsill, the window flung wide open. Her whole body convulsed as she cried out against the mountain wind.

The witch? Huh?

Her wailing was so heart-wrenching, I had to remind myself how she had treated me and Caleb to stop myself from going up to her and asking her what on earth was wrong. I had never expected such a creature could experience sorrow and grief. Even the witches back at The Shade were guarded with their emotions. So to see this woman howling disturbed me deeply.

I stood dumbstruck for several minutes. I was knocked to my senses only when footsteps came down the main staircase. I scrambled away in time to see three male vampires descend into the entrance hall and walk straight through to the dining room. I climbed back up the stairs and returned to my apartment.

Shivering, I jumped into bed and curled up beneath the blankets, the witch's wails still echoing in my head. Her grief reached into the marrow of my bones.

Whatever and wherever this place is, its halls are haunted with sorrow and pain.

I miss The Shade.

I miss home.

Chapter 22: Rose

The noises started again soon after midnight. I tried blocking my ears with my hands and curling up in a ball, but I couldn't stop the sounds from trickling through into my ear drums, disturbing me enough to ensure that night would yet again be sleepless.

I pulled on a dress and my coat and rushed out of the room. I crept up the stairs once again but this time, instead of opening the door, I sat down in a corner of the corridor, outside the room, beneath the shadow of a tapestry hanging on the wall. My imagination ran wild with images of what could be going on in there.

When the door handle finally turned, I held my breath as

the witch exited, her hair disheveled, her dress awry. Once she had disappeared down the corridor, I stood up and eased Caleb's door open. I slid inside and closed it behind me.

I crept along the wrecked corridor and peeked around the corner.

The balcony doors were open, the curtains blowing in the wind. I walked over to them and pulled them aside to see Caleb standing in the cold, leaning against the banister, his muscled back bare and scarred with bloody cuts.

I couldn't help but gasp. But although he must have heard it, he didn't turn around.

I stood next to him and looked up at his face. His eyes were fixed on the horizon, where the ocean sparkled beneath the light of the moon.

I was at a loss for what to say to him anymore. He didn't respond to my questions about anything that was going on. I questioned why I even came up here. Somehow, after I'd heard the noises from the witch's visit, I just couldn't ignore it and go back to sleep as if nothing had happened. I had wanted to see his face. Look him in the eye. So instead I found myself mumbling, "Did you bring me these?" I indicated to my dress and coat.

"Frieda," he muttered, without looking down at me.

"But you asked her to?"

He breathed out and shivered. He walked back into the

room. I followed him, closing the balcony doors behind us.

He took a seat in his wooden chair, but this time he didn't reach for liquor.

"Thank you, is what I was going to say if you'd have given me the chance," I said, crossing my arms across my chest. I paused, then, still eyeing him closely, said, "Would you like me to play for you again?"

From the blank expression on his face, he hadn't heard. But then he shook his head.

"Oh. OK," I said.

I sat down on the bed opposite him and dropped the coat down over my shoulders, staring at him. The bloody cuts on his torso and back were beginning to heal.

"Why did you come here?" he said, standing up abruptly and making eye contact with me for the first time.

Maybe he was just drunk last night when he indicated he'd like to see me again.

His eyes were so intense as they bored into mine, it felt as though I might melt beneath them. But I stood my ground. "So you want me to leave? Is that what you're saying?" I stared up at him, my eyebrows raised in challenge.

He glared at me. I glared back harder.

He sat back down.

"You know, you don't exactly strike me as the happiest of sorts," I said, my hands on my hips as I continued glaring at him. "A little smiling never did anyone any harm."

Whoa. I sound like my mother. She always was Little Miss Sunshine.

A bitter smile curled at the corner of his lips, then he breathed out a sigh and relaxed a little, his jaw becoming less tense.

"So," he said after a few moments. "You want to play for me again?"

"If that's what you'd like."

He nodded. "All right… Rose." He swiveled in his chair so that he was facing the lounge.

His eyes followed me as I walked over to the instruments. This time, I didn't sit down at the piano. I rummaged around until I reached a large instrument which I suspected to be a harp. I pulled off its cover and was pleased to see that my assumption had been correct.

Wiping away the dust from the strings, I sat down on the bench and placed the harp between my legs. I began to strum a melody.

His eyes never left me the whole time I was playing. I could have sworn that his foot tapped slightly to the beat. After I'd grown tired of playing the harp, I moved on to the violin. Then the guitar. Then I sat back down at the piano.

As I started playing the keys, Caleb stood up abruptly. Crossing the room, he sat next to me on the bench. I stopped playing and looked up at him.

"No," he whispered, shaking his head. "Don't stop."

Still eyeing him, I continued playing. He stretched out his fingers on the keys of the upper portion of the piano and began playing the perfect accompaniment to my tune. He played as though he knew it by heart. He barely even looked up at the music sheet.

When the piece finished, my hands slid off the keys and I looked at him, my mouth hanging open.

He stared down at the piano, as though he was as surprised as I was by what he'd just done.

"That's the first time I've touched an instrument in a long time," he breathed.

"Caleb, that was stunning."

I reached out and placed a hand on his shoulder. He flinched as soon as my fingers touched his bare skin.

"I'm sorry, did I hurt—"

"No. No," he muttered, even as he shot to his feet and walked back across the room to his wooden seat.

I stood up too.

We stared at each other from across the room.

I don't know what to make of this man.

Feeling uncomfortable under his gaze, I averted my eyes and looked around the room. It was then, hidden away in a corner, that I spotted something out of place. It was a stereo player. I walked over to it and ran my fingers along its ledge. Beneath it were stacks of CDs.

So maybe this is how he practices his dance moves.

I fingered through the CDs. He had a lot of blues and instrumental stuff. At least, it was more modern than the stuff my dad had brought me up on. *Hmm, but nothing you'd dance to in a nightclub. There goes my theory then.*

"You have a lot of music over here," I remarked.

He nodded.

I picked out a CD and pushed it into the machine. I turned up the volume and stood up once it had started playing.

"So... do you want to, uh, dance again?"

He shook his head, the shadow of a smile crossing his face, and leaned further back in his chair. "I'll watch you."

I snorted. "Oh, yeah? I can't dance."

"You seemed to dance fairly well before."

"Because you were guiding my every movement."

He didn't seem to have a response to that. He just nodded slightly and looked down at the floor.

I walked back over to his side of the apartment and sat down on the edge of the bed.

"It's late. I guess I'll go back to my room now."

"All right."

He remained still, his eyes remaining on the floor, his

body tense again. I was about to reach out a hand for him to shake it, but recalled the time I'd tried to touch him before and thought better of it. Instead I just said, "Good night."

When he didn't even respond to that, I picked up my coat, put my slippers back on and headed out the door.

But just as I was closing the door, I caught him whispering:

"Good night, Rose."

Chapter 23: Caleb

Rose Novak was everything that I wasn't.

Innocent. Vibrant. Untouched.

She was like a patch of fresh snow among the black ice that was the rest of my life.

I didn't want anything or anyone to make a mark on it. Least of all myself.

So when she'd tried to touch me with her soft warm hand, I'd recoiled.

When she'd tried to dance with me, I'd rejected her.

Whenever she'd pressed for answers about me and this castle, I'd brushed her off.

I wasn't refusing to answer her because I wanted to keep

her in the dark. I wanted to keep her *out* of the dark.

I'd just wanted to lock her away. Away from me. Away from Annora.

I didn't want to tarnish her mind with the things that went on in my shadowy world.

But that night, I didn't know why I was in such a good mood. Perhaps it was because Annora had told me she was leaving to visit Stellan's island for a while. Whatever the reason, after I was sure that Rose had fallen asleep, I allowed myself to climb down onto her balcony.

As I caught a glimpse of her peaceful face through the curtains, her expression brought out an ache in me. An ache that both disturbed me and made me feel alive.

I recalled the time I had first laid eyes on her beauty, her face sweaty, her hair disheveled, breath smelling of champagne. She'd behaved like any other teenage girl looking for a night out.

Then she'd told me her name.

And I'd dropped her faster than a hot iron.

I'd heard rumors about the princess of The Shade—not just her beauty, but her innocence, her purity, her light. She was like her mother, they said.

I didn't want to be responsible for ruining that.

I was responsible for enough evil already.

And now that she was on the island, since I couldn't allow

her to leave—at least for the time being—I swore that I would do my best to shield her from her surroundings.

The truth was, I wasn't so much afraid of Derek Novak as I was of breaking his daughter.

Chapter 24: Ben

I'd been injected with something shortly after Stellan pulled me back into the submarine and I'd woken up in this dark dungeon. I'd lost track of how much time had passed since then.

I looked around the prison at the other cells, all crammed with humans. I was the only one to have been given my own cell.

My eyes fell on Kristal and Jake behind the gate across the corridor from me. Jake was lying on the floor in the corner, Kristal huddled up next to him, trying to get some sleep. The vampires who had come in to leave us water and bread had refused to answer any questions.

I just hope that Rose is somewhere better than this.

"Kristal!" I hissed through the bars. "Kristal."

A few humans stirred and looked up at me. But Kristal remained lying still. One of the humans nudged her, bringing her to consciousness.

She rubbed her eyes wearily. Terror set in again on her face after her reprieve. She crawled over to the bars and stared at me. "Has anything happened since I fell asleep?"

I shook my head. Her whole body was shivering. It was freezing down in these dungeons and they hadn't given us enough blankets.

She gripped the bars tighter, leaning her head against them. Tears spilled down her cheeks.

"What are they going to do with us, Ben?"

I'd already explained to both of them that our kidnappers were vampires. They'd had a hard time getting used to that idea—and I was sure Jake still thought I was a raving lunatic. They'd never been exposed to any supernatural creatures before, so I couldn't have expected a different reaction from them.

Jake suspected that maybe we'd been taken for ransom because of their wealthy father.

"If these people really are...v-vampires," Kristal continued, "what would they want with us?"

The answer would have been too troubling for her to hear

in her already weakened state, so I just shrugged. She, however, wasn't going to accept that for an answer.

"Is it our blood that they want?"

I breathed out, unsure of whether to answer.

She read my silence and clasped a palm over her mouth, trembling more than ever.

"Kristal," I whispered. "Look at me."

She raised her bloodshot eyes to mine.

"What's that at the back of your cell?" I asked, pointing at something I'd spotted piled up on the floor.

She turned around and crawled toward it, trying not to wake her cell mates who were blocking her path.

"It's just a pile of chains," she murmured.

"Can you throw them to me?"

She picked the chains and crawled back over to the bars. Gathering them in one hand, she reached through the bars and swung them toward me. I managed to catch them before they clattered to the floor.

There was a padlock fixed to one of the metal joints, but no sign of the key. This appeared to be the kind of padlock that locked without a key by pushing it until it clicked.

I sat for the next few hours leaning against the bars, waiting with bated breath for the dungeon door opening. A vampire was due to come in at any time now to bring us our daily food and water.

Perhaps it was just my nerves playing tricks on me, but the vampire seemed to come in much later that day. Eventually, the door unlatched and heavy footsteps approached.

A vampire pushed along a trolley, passing out water jugs and bread. I tried to keep my breathing steady as he stopped outside my cell. He bent down low, pushing the water and bread through my bars. He stood up and before he could continue, I reached through the bars and slipped the chain around his neck.

He gasped in shock and let go of the trolley. I yanked the chain back with all the strength my weak, dehydrated body could muster and pressed against the padlock. It clicked as he thrashed about.

His razor-sharp claws caught my cheek, ripping open a gash. I ducked down and removed the cluster of keys attached to his belt.

The whole gate shook from his struggling. I didn't have long. I fumbled with the keys until I'd found the one to open my gate. Then I rushed over to Kristal's cell and unlocked it, freeing all the humans who were inside it along with Jake. I did the same with every other cell along that corridor.

"Follow me," I hissed once they'd all bundled out. "Don't make a sound."

I had no idea where I was taking them. For all I knew, I could have been leading us all to our deaths. But something told me that if we didn't try to escape at the first opportunity that came our way, we'd regret it.

"Wait here," I whispered, as we approached the dungeon's exit. I peered around the door to see that it led to a staircase leading upward. There was nobody in sight. "Okay, follow me."

I paused again once I reached the top of the stairs. We were now in some kind of kitchen—metal tables lined the room and in the corner stood jugs filled with a red liquid. *Human blood.*

Kristal's trembling hand gripped my own.

"What is this place?" she gasped.

I held a finger to my lips. I walked along the edge of the room to the nearest exit.

The door was ajar. As I peeked through the crack, my breath hitched. Two vampires stood talking to each other in the center of a large dark hall.

I gestured urgently at the humans behind me to hide underneath the tables. I needed them out of the way while I figured out the best way to escape. With hindsight, I should have let them out of their cells only once I'd found a way out. It would have been less noticeable in case a vampire went down to the dungeon. But it was too late now for regrets.

Hiding under the tables wouldn't do much good if they came in. I knew the vampires would smell our blood, but I hoped that it would be masked at least somewhat by the jugs of blood already sitting on the table in the corner of that room.

Once everyone had hidden themselves, I walked back to the dungeon door and pushed it closed as noiselessly as I could.

I walked to the door at the other end of the kitchen. Opening the door, I found myself looking around another high-ceilinged hall. This one was empty.

I crossed the hall and reached the other side, hiding in the shadows of the doorway. The next room appeared to be some kind of library. Bookshelves lined the walls and there was a round table in the center with tall piles of books.

I had just about reached the other side of the room when someone spoke.

"Can I help?"

Behind one of the large piles of books, a tall thin woman stood up. She had long black hair and cold grey eyes.

"Oh," she said, scowling at me.

I rushed out of the door and into the next hall, only to find the same woman standing there, blocking my path.

This is a witch.

She reached up and gripped my ear, tugging me down to her level. As her fingers touched my skin, a burning sensation rushed through me.

I had to bite my lip to not shout out in pain.

"Where do you think you're going? Stellan!" she shouted, her voice echoing around the room. "Stellan, come here this instant."

No.

The ginger vampire who had pulled me through the hatch came rushing into the hall. His mouth dropped open when he saw me.

"What?" he gasped.

"Looks like you need to tighten up on security," she said.

Stellan's eyes darkened and he gripped me by the neck, dragging me back through the hallways. I struggled against him, but he kneed me in the gut, winding me. His hold was far too strong for a mere mortal to escape from.

He dragged me back into the kitchen and as soon as we entered, Kristal came rushing out of her hiding place.

"No! Ben!"

"No!" I yelled, pushing her back.

It was too late. She'd just given the game away.

Stellan's voice boomed through the kitchen as he called for backup.

Five vampires ran into the kitchen and began pulling out

humans from under the table. A sixth vampire came running into the room with chains. They lined the humans up against the wall and tied them up.

The witch entered the room behind me, eyeing Kristal, who had tears streaming down her face.

"Hm. Interesting," the witch said softly.

She grabbed Kristal by the hair and forced her to the floor.

"I say we teach this young Novak a lesson," she said. "Seeing that he might be with us for quite a while, if he plans to make attempting escape a habit, it will become very tiresome indeed."

The vampires stopped what they were doing and looked over at us, Stellan's grip on me unrelenting.

The witch withdrew a dagger from her cloak and held it against Kristal's neck.

"No!" I yelled, managing to break free from Stellan, only to have three vampires throw themselves at me to hold me down. Stellan lifted my head to face Kristal's trembling form. Jake shouted and struggled against his chains.

"Watch," Stellan grunted, holding my head in position.

With one sharp motion, the witch drove the dagger into Kristal's chest. Her scream was stifled as she choked on her own blood. Both my and Jake's yells echoed around the kitchen as she bled to death in front of us.

"Now," the witch said, letting go of Kristal's hair. "Let this be a lesson to all of you. Stellan. Have your men collect her blood."

Chapter 25: Rose

I was woken the next morning by another knock at my door.

What is it this time?

I found myself looking at Caleb's harp. I supposed he'd thought it would give me something to do while I was alone in my room for hours. I felt grateful for the gesture. Then my eyes settled on the floor beside the instrument. A tray full of food. Not oatmeal. Real breakfast food. I pulled the harp into my bedroom. Then I returned to scoop up the tray and put it on my bedside table, and began to eat hungrily. French toast had never tasted so good to me in all my life. I gobbled everything up in less than five minutes.

I wonder where on earth Frieda—Caleb—even got this food?

I witnessed for myself how bare the kitchen was.

Once I'd finished, I took a shower and got dressed.

I headed up the stairs toward Caleb's room. I knocked on the door and waited. He answered it after a couple of minutes, appearing at the door fully dressed, no trace of the scars from the previous night left visible.

"I, uh. I wondered if you'd mind taking me for a walk? Outside, I mean. I haven't had any proper exercise in days."

He stared down at me, a flicker of discomfort showing across his face, followed by indecision. I thought he was about to say no, but then he nodded.

"All right," he said. "Wait here."

He returned a few seconds later wearing shoes and holding a scarf in his hands.

I eyed the scarf as he stepped out of the room and shut the door behind him.

"I didn't know vampires needed…"

He handed it to me before I finished my sentence. "For you. It's freezing out there."

"Oh. Cheers." I took it and wrapped it around my bare neck.

He gestured toward the stairs and I followed him.

"Thanks for the harp. And the breakfast."

Keeping his eyes straight ahead, he nodded slightly.

We descended the stairs in silence. When we reached the

main door, he pulled a key from his pocket and unlocked it. Pushing with both hands, he heaved the doors open. The force of the icy wind that came flooding through the doorway knocked me breathless.

"Can you manage?" he asked, frowning.

"Yes," I said immediately. *As if I can't walk through a bit of wind without his help.*

Holding onto the door for support—my eyes now beginning to water from the wind—I walked to the edge of the wide stone doorstep and, rather too brashly, placed one slippered foot onto the icy ground. It started sliding as soon as I made contact with it.

I can do this. I just need to take it slowly...

I placed the second foot on the ground and found enough confidence to let go of the door completely.

Swiveling around, I turned myself to face Caleb, who was watching me, his expression blank. Glancing down the side of the mountain, I was so taken by the sheer beauty of the frozen landscape, I lost concentration and slipped. Just as I was about to make contact with the ice, Caleb's arms wrapped around me, breaking my fall.

His face inches from my own, I could feel his cool breath against my cheek as he pulled me upright.

Okay, these slippers weren't designed for the Antarctic.

"So that witch," I said, clearing my throat and looping an

arm firmly though his, "Annora. She makes this island freezing like this just to make it more difficult for the humans to escape?"

"That's the main reason."

"And you have to put up with this weather all year round. What an asshole."

Caleb didn't respond to my outburst, though I could have sworn I saw the shadow of a smile on his lips.

I gripped onto him as we began to make our way down the narrow steps.

"So, what's your name?" I asked.

"You know my name."

"Your full name."

"Caleb… Achilles."

"Achilles? As in the tragic Greek hero Achilles?"

I was about to say "as in the Brad Pitt Achilles". But I wasn't sure if he would have seen that movie. I wasn't sure if he even watched movies.

"It's also a Germanic surname."

"Oh. I see."

I started wondering about what his boundaries were in terms of questions he would answer. *I suppose there's only one way to find out.*

"Do you have family?"

He shook his head, his eyes fixed on the icy steps.

"How old are you?"

"Nineteen."

"And how long ago were you turned?"

"A while ago."

Hm.

"So when you're not out kidnapping girls, you're moping around this gloomy old castle?"

"You could put it like that."

No wonder you're depressed.

By now I was beginning to get tired of walking down the steps in my slippers. "Would you carry me the rest of the way down?"

He grunted and scooped me up in his arms. Then he began dashing down the mountain. My eyes watered from his speed coupled with the fierce wind blowing against us. I half expected him to slip and for both of us to go tumbling down the mountainside, but he didn't falter once. Every step was perfect.

He placed me down again once we reached the bottom of the mountain. Feeling more confident on this flat surface, I didn't reach for his arm again as we walked toward the entrance of the woods.

"So," I said. "I take it that you don't have a girlfriend?"

No duh, Captain Obvious. Unless she doesn't mind taking a bedtime beating alongside him every night when the witch comes to visit.

"You'd be correct in assuming that."

Change the subject.

"So how did you know about me?"

He glanced down at me, an eyebrow raised.

"You seemed to know who I was the moment I mentioned my name back on the beach."

He ran a hand through his hair and clenched his jaw. "Most vampires have heard of you," he muttered. "You're princess of The Shade. That place is a legend."

"Have you ever visited The Shade?"

He shook his head.

"It's beautiful. Much nicer than this bleak place. Why don't you come live with us there instead? We could leave now. I'd make sure that my parents welcomed you and—"

Exhaling sharply, he broke away from me and ran to a nearby tree. Ripping off a thick branch, he snapped it in two over his knee. Then he rested his arm against the tree, his back still turned to me, his whole body heaving.

"Caleb?" I whispered.

He turned back round to face me, composing himself again and standing up straight, his face once again unreadable.

"We should return."

Chapter 26: Rose

Annora.

I need to understand what's going on between her and Caleb. I don't know how or why, but I'm certain that she's what's preventing Caleb from helping me escape this island.

I lay awake in bed late that night once again, expecting to hear the commotion start upstairs as soon as midnight struck. But there was nothing. I waited until one o'clock, and when I still heard nothing, I climbed out of bed, pulled on my coat and slippers, and crept out of the door.

What does this mean? She's visited him every single evening ever since I got here. Why not tonight?

I crept up to Caleb's floor and stood outside his

apartment. Placing my ear to the door, I tried to catch any indication that the witch could be in there.

But the whole castle was deathly silent.

Instead of returning to my room, I took the staircase leading up to the witch's apartment. As I reached the red-carpeted landing, I was taken aback to see that her front door was open. Looking around me, my breathing quickening, I peeked inside. The entrance hall appeared empty, so I stepped in. I walked around the room, running a hand along the dusty wooden furniture as I looked around.

Finding nothing of interest, I moved into the adjoining room. Again empty.

This appeared to be a dining room. Shelves lined the walls, mostly containing books with a strange language scrawled down their spines.

Glass clinked. Dropping to the floor, I crawled toward the door at the opposite end of the room. It was ajar, light emanating through, along with a chilly draft.

Barely daring to breathe, I peeked through the crack. I was expecting to see the witch. Instead, sitting on the carpet in the center of the room was Caleb.

The window was wide open, an icy breeze blowing through the room. He had a glass of blood by his side and an old oak chest open in front of him on the floor. He was sifting through it slowly, lifting out a few random objects—a white pearl necklace, a gold ring, and what appeared to be a dried-up bouquet of flowers.

He placed them all down in front of him on the carpet. His eyes were distant as he gazed down at them, as though lost in thought.

He picked up the ring again and rolled it between his thumb and forefinger. As if it had just burnt him, he dashed it against the floor and, picking up his glass of blood, hurled it against the mirror. It shattered, blood dripping down the mirror onto the wooden cabinet beneath it.

I sneezed.

The chilly breeze had gotten to me. I swore beneath my breath.

When he turned toward me, I slid away from the door and climbed under the table.

The door creaked open, and his feet paced along the edge of the table. He sniffed the air.

Oh, no.

He can smell my blood.

I scrambled further back, careful to keep beneath the tablecloth.

His footsteps approached closer and closer until I could crawl back no further. I held my breath as his feet stopped just inches away from where I was curled up.

His hand reached down and pulled up the tablecloth.

His face didn't appear, but the game was over because my legs were now visible.

He drew in a deep breath. Then he reached down once again, this time gripping my arm as he yanked me out from under the table and pulled me to my feet.

"What are you doing here?" he growled, his dark brown eyes narrowing on me.

I averted my eyes to the floor. He gripped me harder and shook me.

"Answer me!"

"I-I saw the witch crying the other day. And I just—"

He slammed my back against a wooden cabinet.

"It's none of your business what goes on here. Do you hear me?" he shouted, pressing me so hard against the wood that it was a struggle to breathe.

When I didn't answer, he released me, though his glare didn't let up.

Trembling, I ran back through the rooms until I reached the exit. I didn't look back as I hurried back down to my apartment.

Tears formed in my eyes as I swung my door open and rushed out onto my balcony. I stood staring out at the starry sky, trying to calm my nerves.

I stood there for far too long in the cold. But as I closed my eyes, the fresh air felt like it was transporting me somewhere else. *Somewhere other than this godforsaken place.*

After about half an hour, the front doors to the castle creaked open. I looked down and watched as a lone figure stepped out onto the icy entrance steps and sat down. Breathing heavily. Head in his hands.

Chapter 27: Rose

I didn't see Caleb again for the next few days. Even if I hadn't come down with the flu and been forced to stay in bed, I would have still avoided him as he avoided me.

I guessed that the flu had been brought on by standing too long on the balcony. I had a headache and didn't feel like eating anything.

When I showed no signs of getting better after the fifth day in bed, I began to worry. It wasn't like there were any doctors on call here. Normally when we got sick, Corrine took care of us. I was too shaken by our last encounter to want to approach Caleb for anything.

So I lay in bed, getting up to stoke the fire every once in a while, and wearing the coat wrapped tightly around me beneath the blanket.

By the seventh day, Caleb must have suspected that something was wrong. Frieda entered my room and walked over to my bed. One look at me, and she hurried back out.

Do I really look that awful?

She returned half an hour later with Caleb. His face appeared hazy as I looked up at him. His cold hand touched my forehead. I experienced some relief the moment his skin touched me. His hand was better than any cold towel.

"She has a fever," he muttered to Frieda. "A very high fever. Stay in this room until I get back. Make sure the fireplace remains hot. This room still feels too cold. Also make sure all the windows are shut tightly."

He walked out of the room and Frieda went about her duties.

I must have drifted off by the time he returned. But I was woken by his cool palm on my forehead once again.

"Sit up," he said.

Frieda propped up cushions behind me and he reached around me as he pulled me into a sitting position. He sat down on the bed next to me and held a metal cup out in front of me.

"You need to drink this."

I stared at it. A strange dark brown substance. Clasping it

in my hands, I sniffed it.

"Ugh," I groaned, nauseated by its pungent smell.

"Drink."

He pushed the cup against my lips, and, supporting the back of my head with his hand, tipped some of the liquid into my mouth.

It burnt the inside of my mouth as soon as it entered, and singed my throat as I swallowed it.

"Ah!" I cried out. "No. No any more. Please don't make me—"

But he was already gripping the back of my head and tipping more of the liquid through my lips.

I choked and complained again, but he ignored all my protests, forcing me to continue drinking until I had downed the very last drop.

"Give her some water now," he said to Frieda.

She handed me a glass of water. I drank it down in a few gulps. Still the foul taste lingered on my tongue. I slid back down beneath the covers and glared up at Caleb.

"What the hell was that?"

"A potion," he said.

"The witch made it?"

He shook his head.

"The witch isn't here right now."

Hm. That would explain a lot.

"Then who?"

"I made it."

I stared up at him. Dancer. Musician. Potion-maker. The more time I spent with this man, the less I felt I knew about him.

"So can you do spells too?"

He shook his head again. "I've just spent enough time around witches to have picked up a trick or two."

He forced me to drink that foul liquid three times a day. He personally made sure that I swallowed every last drop. As revolting as it was, I couldn't deny that each time I drank it, I felt better. By the third evening, my appetite had returned to normal and I was able to walk around again.

He sat in the chair in the corner of my room, watching me stretch my legs.

"Rose," he said, breaking the silence after Frieda had left us. "I apologize if I hurt you the other night."

My hands reached instinctively for my shoulders as I recalled the incident. He had not so much hurt me as shaken me.

I nodded.

"All right."

He stood up and headed toward the door. Before opening it, he turned around to me.

"You need to understand that there are things that I

cannot and will not talk about with you. There are many things about me, the witch, and this place that you cannot know. So you need to stop pressing me for answers. But you have my word that I will do what I can to get you out of here as soon as the next opportunity presents itself. I want you out from under my skin just as much as you want out of here. I can't tell you when or how it will happen, but you have my word: I will be waiting and watching for that time."

With that, he left and shut the door behind him.

Chapter 28: Rose

With Caleb's assurance, it felt as though a weight had been lifted off my shoulders. I still had no idea when or how I would escape, but somehow I trusted Caleb. Despite his mood swings and unpredictable nature, there was something in his eyes that was sincere.

I also couldn't deny that all along he had shown no signs of wanting to keep me trapped here. Indeed, he had left me behind on the beach when he could have easily taken me. Even though I didn't understand why he couldn't help me escape now, he had gone out of his way to try to save both Ben and I. He'd risked his life and those of his men in ambushing Stellan and trying to save us. I was quite certain that he would have returned us immediately to The Shade.

The witch deserved my resentment. But not Caleb. The man seemed to be bearing enough weight on his shoulders without my resentment.

No, he deserved more than that from me.

I had tried to pry but it had just earned me his ire. I just had to trust that he would help me to escape as soon as he could.

The following evening as I was getting out of the shower and drying my hair, the oak doors creaked open below my balcony. I wrapped the coat around me and looked down over the banister.

Caleb sat on the stone steps, staring out over the frozen dark island and the sea beyond.

I hurriedly got dressed, dried my hair as best as I could, and left the room. I rushed down the stairs until I hurried across the entrance hall.

"Caleb," I said, placing a hand on his shoulder as I reached the snow-covered steps.

He didn't flinch at my touch as I had expected him to. I sat down next to him in the snow.

"Thank you," I said softly.

He stared at me, his expression hard to read, as though he wasn't sure how he should be reacting to my expression of gratitude.

He cleared his throat. "I don't know why you would thank me."

I sighed, averting my eyes to the beautiful view surrounding us.

"You tried to save Ben and I from Stellan," I said. "You've looked out for me ever since I got here. You just nursed me back to health. Look, I don't know what this place is, Caleb. But it honestly feels like you're the only light I have here. Guiding me. Making me believe that there's still hope I might escape. Just thinking about what I'd do if you weren't here…" I shuddered and turned to face him again. "Just thank you, okay? For being my light during this long, dark night."

His eyes widened and his lips parted, as though he was going to say something. But then he glanced away from me and looked back out at the view.

I moved closer to him on the step and, lifting his arm up, placed it around my waist. He tensed up, but I didn't move away. I rested my head against his shoulder, settling myself in closer against the contours of his body.

"A vampire has never felt warmer to me than you do right now," I whispered.

Chapter 29: Caleb

For being my light during this long, dark night.

Her words replayed in my mind long after she had spoken them.

Me? Her light?

The words sounded so preposterous, at first I'd thought that she was joking. But when I'd looked down into those beautiful green eyes of hers, I'd seen earnestness behind them.

I hadn't known what to do or say as she wrapped my arm around her small waist. And when her warm body pressed closer against me, my muscles tensed as her nearness overwhelmed my senses.

After she showed no signs of moving from her position, I felt concerned that my coldness was starting to drain the warmth from her.

"I don't want you getting sick again," I muttered.

I removed my arm from her waist and, taking both her hands in mine, pulled her to her feet.

Still holding her hand, I led her inside the hall. I reached into my pocket and locked the doors.

When I turned around, she reached her arms up around my neck, requesting that I carry her. I obliged, swallowing hard as I glanced down at her soft neck, mere inches from my mouth.

I placed her down outside her room and turned to leave, but she caught my hand and tugged on it.

"I never asked you to return me to my room," she said, a shy smile lighting up her face. "It's not my bedtime yet."

My stomach writhed as she started running up the stairs toward my room, pulling me along behind her.

Once we reached my level, she ran along the corridor and pushed open my unlocked door. Still holding my hand, she pulled me through the hallway until we reached my bedroom.

She slipped off her coat, revealing an emerald-green dress that clung to her delicate curves. Still wearing her slippers, she walked over to the CD player in my lounge.

"Rose?"

She glanced back over her shoulder innocently, looking up at me through her long dark lashes.

"Yes?"

"What are you doing?"

She didn't answer until she'd pushed a CD into the machine and turned up the volume. She walked over to me and, grabbing my hands once again, tugged at me to join her in the center of the living room.

"Being *your* light." She smiled.

If only you knew how much you already are.

"Dance with me," she said, laughing. "Come on."

I hesitated, staring down at her.

"You were never this shy before when I asked you to dance." She wrapped her arms around my shoulders, drawing herself closer against me. I tensed again at her closeness.

"Come on, Mr Achilles," she whispered, gazing up at me. "You know I'm hopeless without you." She brushed her fingers through my hair.

Slowly, I allowed my hands to slide down her back and settle on her waist. I felt goosebumps as I touched her.

"Teach me," she coaxed.

She began moving against me. I went slow at first, watching her as she moved her feet, making sure I wasn't going too fast. But as the music picked up, I stopped being so concerned since she seemed to be coping with my speed just fine. I raised my eyes to her smiling face. That drew out a smile from my own lips.

"You make me look like I've been dancing all my life," she laughed.

"I do?"

She nodded.

Then she pulled herself up toward me.

Her soft lips caressed my cheek.

My cold, pale cheek.

Chapter 30: Rose

I couldn't keep the smile off of my face as Caleb led me into a dance. He was so gentle. So hesitant at first. I found it endearing.

I wasn't sure what made me reach up and kiss his cheek. It was almost as if I wanted to reassure him, to set him free from whatever doubts were holding him back.

He didn't deserve the life he'd been dealt with. Caleb was a good man. That much was clear to me by now. I wanted to warm him as he'd warmed me.

Once we'd finished dancing, I withdrew my arms from his shoulders. He stepped away from me, though his eyes were still fixed on me. I smiled at his seriousness.

Turning around, I scanned the rest of his apartment. I looked at the ripped wallpaper, the damaged furniture, the smashed mirrors. I walked up to the wall and ran my finger over a torn oil painting.

I turned back to face him, his eyes still following me. I cleared my throat, steeling myself for his response. "You don't have to live like this, you know."

He heaved a sigh and turned his back on me. "Don't," he muttered.

"I don't know you, Caleb," I continued. "But I don't think that you belong in this castle."

He remained still, his breathing heavier as I spoke.

"I promise that I'm not just saying this because I want you to take me home. I'm being honest. Even after witnessing what you do along with these other vampires...I just don't know. There's something I'm not seeing in you that I *should* be seeing in you."

I walked up to him. He avoided my gaze, though he didn't change his stance.

"I'm not asking you to tell me what goes on here. I guess I'm just asking you to stop treating your life like it's worth nothing."

I reached out and touched his arm, hoping that he would look at me and see honesty in my eyes.

"I think you deserve more than this," I said, gesturing

around at the broken-up room. "And if there's some way that I can help… Well, I guess I'm here."

I shrugged when he still didn't say anything. My shoulders sagged and I walked back over to the other side of his room, sitting down on the edge of his bed. He walked over to his piano and sat down, running his fingers over the keys.

"Rose," he said, heaving a sigh. "Sometimes, choices you've made in the past limit the choices you have today."

"Maybe," I replied. "But there is always choice."

He didn't argue back. Instead, he began playing the piano. But he appeared agitated, his fingers flying off the keys as the tone of his music turned aggressive. He stopped abruptly mid-tune. He shot to his feet and glared down at me.

"I want to show you something," he said.

He marched out the room, and I had to run behind him to keep up.

He walked straight out of his apartment and took a sharp right turn, walking along the corridor until we reached the stairs. To my surprise, he grabbed my hand and pulled me up toward the witch's level. He opened her apartment door and, pulling me through the different rooms, stopped in the same room where I'd spied on him sitting with the wooden chest.

He walked over to a table and lit four candles. Then he approached a cabinet in the corner of the room and pulled out what appeared to be an old leather-bound photo album.

"Come here," he ordered.

I approached the table. He finished flipping the pages somewhere in the center of the binder and dropped it down on the table in front of me.

Spread out over two pages were four fading black and white photographs.

I gripped the binder and lent closer to the photos. Each were of the same young couple—a young man and a woman. I brushed my fingers over the photographs, clearing away the dust, and as I did, I couldn't stop myself from gasping.

The four photographs were of a young man and woman standing at the helm of a boat—clearly taken on the same day, since they were both wearing the same outfits in the photos: the girl, a flowing summer dress; the man, a casual shirt, sleeves rolled up to his elbows, and pants. Both smiling, they had their arms around each other, embracing like lovers.

The man was clearly a once-human Caleb.

And the woman… long black hair, tall, slim… the witch. Annora.

"That was my choice," he said, his deep brown irises glistening in the candlelight. "Do you understand?"

Chapter 31: Caleb

I didn't take my eyes off of my beautiful captive as she stared at the photographs.

She gazed up at me after a few minutes. "You two were lovers?"

I nodded, picking up the photo album and placing it back on the shelf. There was only so long I could stand having that album open.

"Oh. Wow."

She sank down in a chair.

"We were engaged at one point," I said, walking around to the opposite side of the table and placing my hands on the table, staring at the engraving in the wood.

"But what happened?"

I sat down in a chair and glanced at her face. Grimacing, I braced myself to recount a history I'd long tried to forget.

I was the son of a shipyard owner. As I was his only child, my father trained me from a young age in vessel construction and repairs. He took pride in being the most reputable shipbuilder in town. All the wealthy merchants and aristocrats would come to us as their first stop whenever they needed a repair or a new ship.

One such client was a silk merchant. He owned a fleet of ships and did regular business with my father. I always looked forward to the time he would call by, because his daughter was often with him.

Annora. She was the most beautiful girl I'd ever laid eyes on. Tall, slim, long black hair flowing down her back, enchanting grey-blue eyes. Each time her father came in with a ship, I would snoop around to see whether she was on board. I was too reserved to talk to her at first. But eventually, I gathered the courage to start conversation. Small talk here and there at first, but she also took a liking to me. Soon she was the one seeking me out whenever they moored in our shipyard.

My attraction to her grew stronger with each meeting. When I think of her now, I can't believe she is the same person. She used to be such an innocent, shy creature. Her gentle nature was intoxicating to me. I found myself craving her presence and wishing our time together was longer. I couldn't get her out of my mind. I even dreamt of her at night.

Our friendship soon turned into a romance and, although her father didn't fully approve of me, since he considered me beneath her, he didn't object either.

After a year of seeing each other, on my nineteenth birthday, I proposed to her. She accepted on the spot and swore that she would love me until her last breath.

We were due to be married in three months. Our families started making arrangements.

Then one evening, my life changed forever.

My father sent me to service the ship of a new client. The client was an exceedingly wealthy saffron merchant who was new to these parts and required exceptional attention. Also, the gentleman had requested that the ship be fixed during the night because of an eye condition that made him sensitive to the sun.

Although I despised doing repairs at night—it was always ten times more difficult than during the day—I agreed to my father's request. Apparently there was a problem with the wheel of the saffron merchant's ship.

"Sir?" I called, as I climbed onto the deck.

There was no answer. I walked along the deck until I reached the captain's compartment. I knocked three times. A tall man opened the door. His eyes were pitch black, and his skin was strangely pale. He appeared to be middle-aged, smartly dressed, his hair slicked back with some kind of expensive-smelling oil.

"Over here," he said, shutting the door behind us and guiding me toward the wheel.

I placed my tools on the floor and began my examination, the shortest of my career. The man walked up close behind me. At first I thought he was just watching what I was doing, but then cold hands gripped my throat and the man dug his teeth into my neck.

I was too stunned to even scream at first, but when I did, nobody could have heard me. The door was closed and his ship was moored in the farthest berth. Soon, I had no more strength to struggle. I writhed on the floor in the heat of transformation.

The man's black eyes flickered in the candlelight as he watched me throughout my transformation.

When the agony burning through my body had begun to subside and I had stopped coughing up blood, he held his hand out to me, helping me to my feet. Still too feeble to stand, I sank down in a chair.

"What is this?" I gasped.

"A gift," he replied, chuckling.

He gripped my bloodstained shirt and threw me off his ship. I lay helpless on the wooden jetty as the saffron merchant's ship sailed away into the distance.

Those next few hours were the most frightening of my entire

life. I didn't know where to go or whom to trust. I had heard rumors of vampires who walked among us. I didn't know many details other than that they were evil creatures.

My first wave of bloodlust hit me, so strong that I realized I couldn't even return to my home without pouncing on my parents and sucking them dry.

I ran as fast as I could toward the beach, away from the town. Away from my family. Away from Annora. I raced for hours along the beach until the sun rose. My skin began to burn so intensely, I thought I was going to die. I ran toward the first cave I could find and hid in its darkest corner. I curled up in a ball, trying to control the way my body was convulsing for want of blood.

I tried to force myself to sleep, to forget the pain and hunger, but it was useless. I stayed in the corner of that cave all day and all night. I remained there for at least five days before a search party came looking for me—a search party consisting of my parents, Annora and her brother.

I was horrified to see them approach the entrance of my cave at night, flaming torches in their hands. I managed by some mercy to restrain myself from jumping on them and instead darted out of the cave. I travelled further along the beach. They had no hope of catching up with me that night. I found another cave and, after filling my body with the blood of a dead shark I'd found along the shore, I retreated for the night.

But they didn't stop trying to follow me. Eventually, after the tenth day, I stopped running. My parents and Annora had found my hiding place once again. I climbed out of the entrance of my cave and sat perched on the rocks above, looking down at them.

And I told them everything.

My parents could barely believe their ears. I had to repeat parts of my story several times before they accepted it.

Annora, on the other hand, just stood silently, tears streaming down her beautiful face. I'd thought the pain of being a vampire was intolerable—but the anguish on my lover's face caused me more agony than my transformation.

For the following weeks, I remained living in caves. My parents stopped trying to persuade me to return home. They accepted that I was too much of a danger.

Annora, on the other hand, didn't stop visiting me. As I begged her to forget about me and move on, she refused.

"I can't leave you, Caleb," she'd said, sobs racking her body. "There's no one else I could ever love."

I tried to be callous toward her. I tried to scare her with my fangs and claws. But no matter what tactic I used, she insisted on staying with me.

Then one night when she came to my cave, after a particularly aggressive argument, she asked me to turn her into a vampire. I laughed in her face and thought that she was joking.

But she was deadly serious.

"You've lost your mind," I shouted, storming out of the cave.

I didn't return until the morning, hoping she would have been gone by then. But she wasn't. She'd sat waiting in the cave for me all night.

She approached me as soon as I entered, gripping her hands in mine.

I jolted back. "How many times do I have to tell you? Don't touch me."

"Turn me," *she whispered, her voice hoarse, her eyes red from crying.*

"Annora, stop it," *I hissed.*

She walked closer to me, the smell of her sweet blood invading my nostrils.

"I don't want a life without you."

"You're young and beautiful. You'll find someone else."

"No!" *She began shaking her head furiously. Then she pulled out a dagger from beneath her cloak and held it to her own throat, its tip denting her skin.*

"What are you doing? Put it down!"

She looked up at me with desperate eyes. "Turn me, my love."

I lunged toward her and wrestled the dagger out of her hands, hurling it out of the cave.

I stood staring at her, unable to believe that she'd just threatened me with her own life. That she'd be willing to give it up so easily.

She broke down sobbing again and ran out of the cave. At first I thought she would retrieve the dagger, but she headed back toward the town.

She didn't come to visit again the next day, nor the day after. A week passed and when she still hadn't returned, I thought that she'd finally heeded my request.

But then, on the eighth night, she came to me again.

I was woken from my slumber by the feeling of a warm, smooth body lying against me. Opening my eyes, to my horror, I realized that it was Annora. She'd stripped herself naked and wrapped herself around me.

As soon as she saw I'd woken, she climbed on top of me, her warm hands pressing down against my bare chest, her long black hair grazing my skin as it hung either side of her shoulders. She gazed down at me through her thick dark lashes.

"No," I gasped.

She lowered herself against me and pressed her lips against mine. She began loosening my pants with one hand, her other hand gripping the base of my neck as she continued to kiss me forcefully. Her scent and the way she touched me sent all my senses into overdrive.

I wanted nothing more than to devour her.

I tried to push her off me, but my resolve was evaporating by the second. Once she'd positioned her neck so that my lips were touching it, I was a lost cause.

I gripped her waist and rolled her off me, slamming her against the ground as I positioned myself on top of her. I sank my fangs deep into her soft neck.

I groaned as her hot, sweet blood flowed into my mouth, lighting my body on fire.

"Caleb," she moaned as she writhed beneath me. "Turn me, my love."

Although my conscience was screaming at me to stop, my body was now beyond the point of return. I took three more deep sucks of her exquisite blood and released my venom into her.

I continued drinking from her until her blood began to taste bitter—her transformation now underway. I pulled away from her and watched as she lay writhing on the ground, screaming with pain and coughing up blood.

What have I done?

I stood dumbstruck as the warmth faded away from her, the dark disease consuming every molecule of her body.

Finally she stopped writhing and lay motionless on the floor.

"Annora?"

I rushed over to her and shook her. Her eyelids fluttered a little. I continued shaking her, shouting her name. Finally, her eyelids shot open, her eyes now a steely grey, nothing like the delicate color they were before.

She reached for my neck and gripped me, her claws digging

into my flesh. She lifted herself up to me and attempted to dig her fangs into my neck.

I pushed her away, pinning her to the ground.

"I need blood," she gasped. "I need blood."

Watching her was like reliving my own turning. The horror of craving another's blood without remorse. Feeling like I'd stop at nothing until I got it.

"I-I'll find blood for you," I stammered.

Grabbing the fisherman's net I'd found while roaming along the beach, I gripped her arm and pulled her out of the cave. I walked with her until we reached the sea. I pulled her into the waters until we were deep enough to catch a decent load of fish.

Now that I still had the taste of Annora's blood in my mouth, fish blood seemed the most disgusting thing in the world to me.

"Annora," I muttered, turning around to face her.

But she was no longer by my side—in fact, with several strong strokes, she had almost reached the shore. Alarmed, I began to swim after her. She jumped out of the water and sprinted along the beach toward the town.

"No!" I yelled and raced out of the water after her.

Her speed almost matched my own, so it wasn't until we were about two miles along the beach that I managed to catch up with her. I threw myself at her and wrestled her to the ground.

"Who goes there?"

Both Annora and I looked up. A young fisherman was

approaching us in the darkness, dragging a net full of eels along the sand.

Annora slipped away from my grasp and hurled herself against the man. By the time I reached her, she'd already dug her fangs deep into the man's throat.

Attempting to rip her apart from him now would be pointless. Her fangs were embedded so deep, she'd have torn through the man's artery. I had no choice but to watch her drain him to death.

When she'd finished, she dropped the corpse on the sand. She looked up at me, wiping the blood away from her face with her bare arm. She gave me an eerie smile.

The glimmer of darkness in her eyes disturbed me more than I could describe. Gone was the innocent girl I'd fallen in love with. In her place was a monster.

I comforted myself that perhaps she would get better with time, once she got more used to her bloodlust. I hoped that her old personality would return.

So over the following days, I did my best to keep her inside the cave at all times. I was afraid to even sleep in case she claimed another victim.

But it was becoming increasingly difficult. Her cravings appeared greater than my own and she was showing no signs of even attempting to control them. When a group of humans approached our area of the beach one night, I knew that it was time to move. But I had no idea where to.

I was beginning to grow desperate when, one night, a ship drew in just outside our cave.

The ship of the saffron merchant.

To this day, I don't know how he managed to find out our location.

He told us he could take us somewhere where other vampires lived away from humans. Away from the threat of being discovered. Although I didn't trust a word that came out of his snake-like mouth, we had no other option than to follow.

He ended up taking us to the Elder's castle—The Blood Keep. I knew we'd made a mistake as soon as we drew up outside the tall black gates. The castle from the outside appeared to be a place of nightmares, and once we stepped inside the nightmares became real.

As it turned out, the Elders didn't want Annora and I to remain in that castle for long. They wanted us out of the human realm entirely.

They wanted us in Cruor. The dark hell that was the realm of the Elders.

I had to pause for a moment as the memories washed over me, the images fresh in my mind as if it was only yesterday. Rose's eyes were glued on me. Her chin resting in her hands, she hung onto my every word, a look of horror mixed with fascination on her face.

I'd told her far more than I had intended to already about myself.

She frowned at me as soon as I had stopped. "So you went to Cruor?"

I nodded.

"What was it like?"

I didn't want to give Rose nightmares, so I refused to give her details. "Suffice it to say, Cruor made Annora much worse. She never returned to her former self."

"How did you escape from there?"

"A group of witches came to visit the Elders one day, and offered a fresh batch of humans in exchange for fifty vampires. We didn't know what they needed us for. We didn't question it. And when three witches came to release us from our dungeon quarters, we all followed them without hesitation."

Rose bit her lower lip and rubbed a palm against her forehead. "And Annora... she's not a vampire now?"

"She is a witch."

"But how?"

I paused, considering how to answer her question. "The witches who came for us were... different."

"Huh?"

"These witches didn't come from The Sanctuary."

"Then where did they come from?"

"They have their own abode outside of the witches' realm."

"But *who* are they?" she asked, frustrated.

"Let's just say that they are a darker breed of witches than you've likely ever come across."

"But...how do they get here? Hell, how did *you* get here? I thought the gates between the human realm and the realm of supernaturals were all closed off years ago."

I almost smiled at her naiveté, but refused to answer. Rose pressed for more information, but I brushed her off.

She sighed and crossed her arms over her chest. "Well then, continue. What happened to Annora?"

My eyes glazed over again as I dug back into my memories.

"We were transported away from Cruor and taken to the witches' residence. During our stay there, Annora became increasingly... involved in the things that went on behind their walls. She embraced their way of living in a way that I never could have predicted. She confessed one day to me that she wanted to become one of them. I tried to make her see the consequences of that action, but she ignored me."

"I didn't know that witches could get rid of vampirism from a person, least of all then turn one into a witch. I thought only the blood of an immune and—"

"As I said, these are not ordinary witches."

"So they made her a witch," Rose said slowly.

"In the end, Annora's desire for their power was too great."

"How on earth did you end up here?"

"The witches have reasons for wanting us here," I said, averting my eyes. "Reasons that I won't disclose to you. Since Annora had gained their trust, and since they knew of her connection to me, they decided that she would be the logical person to oversee Stellan and myself running these two islands."

"And all of the vampires here on these two islands—all of them were rescued from Cruor by the witches?"

"Yes. All of us. In exchange for protection from the Elders, we swore an oath to do their bidding."

She breathed out and sat back in her chair, running a hand through her hair.

"So you're all prisoners here?"

"You could put it that way."

"What if you tried to escape?"

"Annora has cast a spell around this island. None of us can leave unless she gives us express permission to do so."

"But when you are allowed to leave—like when you go out hunting for humans—why don't you escape then?"

"We are... bound to these two islands. Any longer than a

week away from them, and…" I paused, remembering the time one of my own men had tried to escape and stayed away for more than seven days. I shuddered as I recalled the state we had found him in.

Rose doesn't need to know these details.

"And what?" she asked.

"We just have to return within a week."

Chapter 32: Rose

I stared at the young man across the table in the dimly lit room. Although he only gave me half answers to every other question I asked, I felt privileged that he was opening up to me in this way.

On several occasions, I wondered why he was revealing all of this to me. What I had done to deserve his trust. His openness. I realized what an ordeal it must have been to recount all of this to me.

The one question that had been burning in my mind ever since I'd laid eyes on the black and white photos of the lovers was now on the tip of my tongue.

"And you and Annora... how did it get this way? Why

does she—"

He held up a hand, and walked slowly to the other side of the room where he stopped, staring out of the window at the snow-covered mountain peaks. He stood still for several minutes and I began to believe that he wasn't going to answer my question. But eventually he cleared his throat and said, "She's sick, Rose."

I remained silent, holding my breath for him to continue.

"I suppose," he said slowly, his back still facing me, "I should have seen where she was heading earlier. I was just too blind."

I stood up and walked over to the window next to him.

"What happens every night when she's here?"

"We fight," he muttered.

"Why?"

"It's..." He paused and bit his lip, as if weighing up his words before he let them roll off his tongue. "It's how she feels alive."

I stared at him disbelievingly. "What?"

He clenched his jaw. It pained me to see how uncomfortable my questions were making him. "It's her way of clinging to the past. To what we used to have."

"What do you mean?"

"She lost her ability to love me the moment she gave herself over to the witches. It's one of the things she sacrificed."

My mind was beginning to reel. I leaned against the wall to steady myself.

"Fighting me... it's the closest she can feel to loving me."

He left me by the window and walked back over to the other side of the room.

"Caleb," I said softly, looking after him. "I think she does still feel for you. I saw her bawling her eyes out."

He shook his head. "She can feel pain, yes. But not love. I learnt that long ago."

Leaning against the wall, I sank to the ground and pulled my knees against my chest.

I didn't know what to say to him. But finally now, it was clear why he put up with her day in and day out.

Caleb feels responsible for what she's become.

Had he not turned her, none of this would have happened.

He thinks he caused her ruin.

"It's late," he said, finally breaking the silence. "I suggest you leave."

Chapter 33: Rose

Caleb stayed away from me after that night.

I didn't seek him out. I wouldn't have known what to say to him if I had.

I stayed locked up in my room and tried to distract myself with music. I now felt doubly grateful that he had sent the harp down to me.

But as much as I tried to put thoughts of the vampire out of my mind, I couldn't. Those old photographs remained etched in my mind, his broken love story replaying over and over in my head.

Most of all, I wondered what would become of Caleb.

Once I escaped from this island, I wondered if this was

how he would live for the rest of his immortal life. I wondered how long he had lived like this already. Bound to this frozen island. Held hostage by the witch's curse and his own guilt.

That man deserves more than this.

Thinking about him made my chest ache with frustration and sadness. And I felt a crushing sense of loss. Loss of what, I didn't understand.

I felt taken aback by the strength of my emotions.

None of this is even my business. I should just be thinking about getting back to my family.

Why do I care so much?

That question haunted me as I tossed and turned in bed in the early hours of the morning. I ended up getting out of bed and walking out on the balcony for some fresh air. I found myself looking up toward his balcony, as if hoping I might see his arms leaning against the banister.

But he wasn't there.

I returned to my bed and just as I was tucking myself beneath the covers, I heard a click. It sounded like the unlatching of my front door.

Caleb?

I got up and approached the hallway. A tall dark figure stood in the doorway.

But it wasn't Caleb.

The figure walked toward me, his face coming further into the dim lighting of my bedroom.

It was the ginger vampire with light blue eyes.

"Stellan," I gasped, stumbling back toward my bed.

A smile crept onto his lips.

"That's right, princess," he whispered. He looked around my room, and an expression of mock relief appeared on his face. "I see there's no hot kettle to help you this time."

"Wh-what are you doing here?"

"Taking you for a little rendezvous."

He launched himself against me, crushing me between his steely arms and flinging me over his shoulder.

"No!" I screamed, lifting both knees and slamming them down against his rock-hard stomach. I was sure that I did more damage to my kneecaps than I ever caused him. I shouted again as loud as I could. Positioning my palms against his lower back, I managed to push myself up enough to wrap an arm around his neck. I pulled tight, pressing against his windpipe and locking him in a choke.

He grunted in frustration and threw me back down against the bed.

"So you want to make this rough, huh?"

He scrambled onto the bed on top of me, pinning both of my arms above my head. Pressing his knees down against my shins, he slid them slowly upward, hiking my dress up my thighs as he moved. He'd stretched my body out so thin, it felt like I couldn't budge an inch without tearing a muscle.

He took my wrists in one hand. His other hand lowered to my face. Claws shot out. He ran a finger against my cheek. I exhaled sharply as he drew blood. His gleaming eyes settled on the blood on my cheek. He groaned, leaning down toward me, his face now barely an inch from my own. His cold tongue ran against my skin, and as soon as it did, his whole body shivered against me.

"What are you doing?" I hissed.

"Taming you a little," he whispered, lowering his eyes to my mouth.

His free hand made its way down to my inner thigh. I clenched my jaw against the pain as he made another mark on me. He loosened his grip around my hands as he lowered his head down toward the fresh blood he'd just shed.

I shot my hand out toward the bedside lamp and, tearing its socket from the wall, smashed it down against his skull.

I was sure that it had done little to hurt him, but it disoriented him enough to give me a few seconds to slide out from under him, roll onto the floor and make a dash for the exit.

I ran out into the corridor and made it to the top of the first staircase before he caught up with me and slammed my back against the wall. His eyes burning with anger, he hurled me back over his shoulder—lowering me down further this time so I had no hope of reaching my arm around him—and began speeding down the stairs.

"Don't take a step further."

Stellan stopped and whirled around.

I couldn't see up the dark staircase from the odd angle I was hanging, but I didn't need vision to know who had spoken.

Stellan chuckled.

"Or what? You'll talk to the witch?"

Heavy footsteps approached us down the steps. They didn't stop until they'd reached us. I caught a glimpse of Caleb's black leather boots.

"Put her down."

"Go to hell," Stellan spat, and started walking down the staircase.

Caleb walked around Stellan and stood on the steps beneath us. His eyes were fixed on Stellan, his face expressionless.

"I won't say it again," he said quietly.

Stellan lowered me to the ground. I groaned as my body made contact with the sharp steps. Stellan remained standing in front of me, blocking me from Caleb.

"Why do you want her so much that you'd defy orders, huh?"

Caleb attempted to walk past Stellan toward me but Stellan reached out and shoved him back.

"You've already had her, haven't you? Now you just don't want to share."

Caleb reached out and gripped Stellan's throat, pinning him back against the wall.

Stellan swiped his claws out and tore against Caleb's chest, dangerously close to his heart. That started a full-on battle between the two men.

I scrambled further up the staircase, out of the way of the two of them as I looked on in horror.

After barely two minutes, both had ripped the skin on their faces and chests to shreds, and although their bodies healed within seconds, the wounds could barely heal fast enough before they were ripped open afresh.

With one strong thrust, Caleb managed to make Stellan lose his footing. Stellan went crashing down to the bottom of the stairs. Caleb launched himself upon him and, gripping his neck while holding his chest down with both knees, snapped it. A loud crack echoed off the walls as Stellan became limp, his eyes vacant.

I knew that he was not dead. Disjointing a vampire's neck just paralyzed them temporarily.

Caleb looked up at me, breathing heavily, his eyes blazing into mine.

"Go back to your room and wait for me." When I hesitated he hissed, "Now!"

I rushed back up the stairs, locking myself in my room.

I had no idea what was happening or what his plan was. Stellan had spoken of the witch's orders. *What orders?*

I'd been waiting for about ten minutes when the door unlatched. Caleb stalked into the room, his skin now almost fully healed from the fight.

Before I could open my mouth to ask questions, he gripped the top of my head and dragged me out of the room by my hair.

"Wh-what are you doing?" I gasped, wincing as his fingers dug into my scalp with each step.

He ignored my question. He pushed open the door and hauled me into the witch's apartment.

I breathed out in pain as he yanked my head upward. As he forced me to my feet, I found myself face to face with the witch.

Chapter 34: Caleb

The witch's cold eyes settled on Rose's distressed face. Then she looked up at me, frowning. "What are you doing with her? I told Stellan—"

"I know what you told Stellan," I said coolly. "But he wants some rest after his last task. I'm doing this instead."

She looked from me to the girl. I made sure to keep my face devoid of emotion—something I'd gotten good at over the years.

Finally, she nodded. "Very well. You have my permission. You know what must be done?"

I nodded and took Rose by the scalp. Pulling harshly enough so that Rose moaned in pain, I dragged her back out of the witch's chambers.

As soon as the door shut, I scooped Rose up in my arms and carried her down the steps. Rose tried to ask me what the hell I was doing, but I ignored her until we'd exited the castle, run down the mountain and reached the port. I set her down at the edge of the frozen jetty while I opened up the hatch of a submarine.

Only once I'd lowered us both inside of it and locked the hatch did I bend down and examine her wounds closely. I swore as I saw how much blood was still oozing from the gashes Stellan had made.

I took her hand and led her into the control room, where I sat her down in one of the seats. She continued to glare at me, her expression full of pain and accusation. I rummaged around in the overhead cupboards until I found a first-aid kit—something we always kept on board, since we transported humans regularly in these vessels.

I bent down next to her and began treating her wounds. I salivated as I wiped up her succulent blood and disposed of the tissues. Once I'd fixed bandages over them, I stood up and looked down at her.

"Rose," I said quietly. "I'm sorry."

She looked up at me, her eyes still wide.

"I had to scare you. The distrust in your eyes helped convince her to let us go."

Her soft lips parted as realization dawned upon her.

"And now?" she asked, her voice hoarse. "Where are you taking me?"

"I'm taking you home."

Chapter 35: Derek

We'd been at a loss for what to do. We had no idea where to even begin looking. And of course the police were even more clueless than us.

We had searched the condo. There had been clear signs of a struggle—the sofa was in disarray, water splashed all over the kitchen, the kettle on the floor along with a knife. A mirror smashed, several paintings fallen off the hooks. The windows had been left wide open—and since there was no record of them leaving the apartment on the CCTV cameras outside of the room, the only conclusion we could come to was that they must have escaped with the four teenagers out of the window. Given the height of the building, unless they had parked a crane alongside it, this wouldn't have been possible for humans.

We saw no choice but to return to The Shade. Hanging around in Hawaii wasn't going to solve anything. We called an urgent meeting in The Great Dome with our closest friends and family. But none of us could figure out what our next step should be. They'd just vanished without a trace.

Now, I was beginning to lose track of how much time had passed since their disappearance. Days merged into a blur. We continued having meetings, but it felt like we were going round in circles.

We'd received no calls from their phone, and whenever we tried calling it, we reached voice mail.

"So we're sure it's vampires behind this, Derek?" Vivienne reached out and clasped my arm.

I looked up into her worried eyes.

"That's the only conclusion we can come to. It's hard to make out their features from the CCTV, but you can see the pale skin beneath their glasses—they definitely look like they could be vampires."

"But why?" Anna sat forward in her seat. "Why would they want the twins?"

"I don't know."

"If they are vampires," Xavier said, "it's possible they targeted the twins on purpose. They may want something from The Shade."

"But what? And how can we even give it to them?"

"Maybe—"

Eli's speculation was interrupted by the sound of a phone ringing.

Sofia reached into her pocket and pulled out our phone.

We all stared at it, dumbstruck.

"Put it on speaker!"

Sofia flipped it open and pressed the speaker button, her hand trembling.

"Rose? Ben?"

No response.

"Hello?" I shouted into the phone.

"My name is Stellan," a deep male voice replied. "And I suggest you listen carefully to what I'm about to say."

My heart leapt into my throat. Sofia gasped and almost dropped the phone. I took the phone from her and laid it down on the table, staring down at it, trying to steady my racing heart.

"We have your twins," Stellan continued. "And they are still alive. How long this will be the case depends entirely on your cooperation."

I wanted to grab the phone from Sofia and shout down the line at this son of a bitch. It took all that I had to stop myself from doing it. Showing emotions would only reinforce their sense of control over us.

"Continue," I grunted.

"We're holding your son and daughter captive. We've given your twins a rough time already, so I suggest that you don't make this more difficult than it needs to be."

"What are you?" Sofia said, her voice weak.

"That's not important. What's important is that you pay attention."

We waited with bated breath for him to continue.

"We know that you hold an immune on your island. In exchange for the return of your children, you will hand over the immune to us."

All eyes shot toward Anna. Blood drained from her face as she sat resting her hands over her pregnant stomach.

I picked up the phone, my resolve disappearing by the second.

"Why do you want an immune?"

"Is that Derek Novak speaking?" The man chuckled. "You know the value of immunes. And since most of them are locked away in the depths of Cruor now, they are almost impossible to find."

"We no longer have the immune," Sofia said. "She passed away a few months ago during labor. But our witches took samples of her blood. We have large stores. We could hand them over to you instead."

Stellan laughed.

"Only the fresh, hot blood of an immune is of use to us. So if your immune has indeed died, then you've nothing to offer us in exchange for the twins. You'd better think long and hard if that immune really is dead."

We all paused, staring at each other. After a few moments, Stellan said, "I'll give you time to think things over and not make any rash decisions, eh? Call me back once you have an answer. You have my number. I'll be waiting."

The phone buzzed as the line cut off.

"They're not getting Anna," almost everyone in the room said at once as soon as the vampire hung up.

I held my hands up for silence. I needed to think fast. Sofia's panicked eyes settled on me.

I sat down in my seat and closed my eyes, resting my head in my hand.

There was no way we would ever hand over Anna. That much was for certain. But we had to find a way to get our twins home unscathed.

I sat for several more minutes in silence as every pair of eyes in the hall bored into me, waiting for my solution.

Finally I looked up. "Hand me the phone."

I dialed our twins' number and waited. Stellan answered after two rings.

"Yes?"

"We do have the immune," I said. "We'll offer her to you in exchange for the twins."

"Hm," he said. "Good. You are to meet us tomorrow night. I suggest you write down the location."

I noted down the details.

"Make sure that immune is with you, Novak. And don't bring any witches. If you breach this agreement, I'll snap the spines of both of your children with my bare hands."

He hung up.

Everyone in the room was looking at me like I'd gone mad.

"What did you just say?" Sofia exclaimed.

"We won't bring Anna with us," I said loudly, quietening everyone's protests. "She will remain here."

"What?" Sofia said.

"We need to turn this into an ambush. We'll bring our best fighters, along with as many witches as we can spare. All we need right now is to have these people within reach. Once we meet them, we won't leave until we've got Rose and Ben safely back with us."

Anna stood up for the first time.

"What if they do something to Rose and Ben once they realize you've tried to deceive them?"

"They won't have time. We'll make this ambush fast. As soon as we lay eyes on them, we'll rush in."

"But we don't even know what Stellan and his companions are," Anna said. "We don't know for sure that they are vampires. How can you be so sure that you'll be able to overpower them and get your twins back?"

"Anna," I said, my chest heaving. "It's our only option."

Everyone quietened down and sat back in their seats.

"So how are we going to go about this exactly?" Xavier asked.

"Listen carefully," I said, flattening my palms on the table as I prepared to voice the plan in my mind.

*****

Vampires and a few witches filled up each of the submarines we had on the island. Sofia and I boarded the smallest submarine alone. We made sure to travel a long distance ahead of the other submarines. We couldn't afford Stellan detecting them.

Eli had given me a pager before we left. He also placed them in each of the submarines. When I pressed mine, the others would take it as a signal to close in.

After a few hours, we arrived at the location. Sofia and I navigated the submarine as close to the beach as possible, and stepped out into the warm night air. A tall vampire with reddish hair was already waiting on the beach. Alone. A few hundred meters away from him was a black submarine.

We approached and stopped a few feet away from him. Looking around the area casually, I couldn't spot other vampires on the beach, and the submarine moored up in front of us appeared to be the only one.

"Where are the twins?" I asked.

"Where's the immune?" he responded.

"We have her in the submarine," I said, reaching into my pocket and pushing the button to signal to our submarines.

"I suggest you bring her out first. Remember, Novak, your twins are worth more to you than the immune is to us."

I nodded and, taking Sofia's hand, returned toward the submarine. We walked as slowly as possible without arising suspicion.

Sofia and I disappeared through the hatch. We exchanged nervous glances. If all went to plan, in less than a minute, an army of our vampires would surface and storm their submarine.

Sure enough, Stellan yelled out into the night air. He rushed back toward his submarine. Sofia and I climbed back out through the hatch and raced after him.

I caught up with Stellan on the sand before he reached the submarine. Leaping forward and gripping his midriff, I tripped him up. He didn't try to fight me. Rather, he scrambled to his feet and ran in the opposite direction. I had almost caught up with him when he ran into the sea—

toward another small submarine that had been hidden from view. He dove through the hatch and slammed it shut before I could climb in after him. Several seconds later, the submarine had submerged beneath the waves.

Confused by his behavior, I returned to the main submarine and, wading through the water, hauled myself up onto its roof and lowered myself through the hatch.

The submarine was in absolute chaos. Vampires at war with each other, lashing out with their claws, biting each other's necks. I caught sight of Sofia fighting a particularly vicious-looking female.

I ducked down beneath the commotion as much as I could. I had to reach Rose and Ben while most of them seemed occupied.

Keeping against the walls, I ran from chamber to chamber until I reached the lower deck. I checked all the rooms down there and stopped outside the only one which was locked. The door was made with reinforced metal.

"Stand back," I shouted through the door to whomever was inside.

I climbed to the top of the stairs and, with all the force I could muster, I smashed down against the door. The impact made a dent in it, but it still didn't open. Again, I struck the door. Now looser. The third time I struck, it swung off the hinges. I hurried inside and looked around the room.

My son lay on the floor, his eyes closed. There was no sign of Rose.

I hauled Ben's body over my shoulder, relieved to feel he was still breathing, and ran out of the room. I looked once more in every corner of the lower deck but Rose was nowhere to be seen. I rushed back up to the top level and barged through the crowds of fighting vampires until I reached the hatch.

As I climbed up, pain seared through my ankle. A vampire dug his claws into me. I shook the vampire off, kicking him in the face. I climbed out of the hatch and jumped into the water. Readjusting Ben's weight over my shoulders, I ran back to our submarine and placed Ben down on top of a blanket in the back of the vessel.

Where the hell is Rose?

My stomach churned as I ran back toward the submarine. We had managed to overpower quite a few of the other vampires already, though many were still fighting against us. I breathed a sigh of relief on seeing no casualties on our side yet.

In the corner Aiden tied up a male vampire in line with a bunch of others we'd managed to tranquilize. I reached out for Aiden's shoulder and he spun round to face me.

"I found Ben," I said. "You need to go to the small submarine immediately. Ben is there. Bring some witches and help care for him."

"And Rose?"

"I haven't found her yet."

As Aiden rushed off, I looked around the vessel for Sofia. I spotted her in the far corner of the room, struggling beneath the weight of a large male vampire.

I gripped his neck between my arms and with one sharp motion I disjointed it. I held out my hand and pulled Sofia off the floor, her face shining with sweat. "I found Ben," I said. "But Rose isn't here."

"What?"

"I searched this whole vessel. She's not here."

I began to fear the worst—that the reason Stellan had fled so quickly was that he held Rose separately from Ben just in case we attempted to pull a stunt. He probably thought that we wouldn't risk an ambush or anything that could put our precious twins' lives in danger. He thought that we would rather just hand over our immune. But just in case we tried an ambush, he kept Rose separately. Thinking now with hindsight, I was kicking myself for not having considered he might do this. He would have been a fool not to.

"But where could she be?"

"We need to find out where it is these vampires reside."

Leaving Sofia's side, I raced over to Xavier, who was just about to inject a vampire with a tranquilizer. I knocked it out of his hands and pulled the vampire away from him. She had a youthful face, possibly in her twenties when she was turned, and short blonde hair.

I outstretched my claws and positioned them over her heart while my other hand gripped her neck. "You are going to take us to your base," I hissed.

I pulled her up and dragged her into the control room. "Where do you vampires come from?"

When she remained silent, I pressed my claws against her throat. She gasped but still didn't speak.

"There are plenty of other vampires I can ask. So I suggest you speak, unless you prefer that I rip your heart out."

"All right," she croaked, gasping. I released the pressure from her neck. "We live on an island, about an hour away from here."

"What island?"

"Stellan rules over it. It's protected by a witch's spell."

"A spell? Will we be able to enter it?"

Trembling, she nodded. "Yes, because you are accompanied by us."

I pushed her into the control seat and said, "Do you know how to operate this thing?"

"Y-yes."

"Then you'll take us there. You said it takes about an hour. I'll be watching the timer. I suggest you don't mess with me."

She eyed my claws as I sat down next to her, ready to strike if I sensed even the slightest bit of disobedience from her.

I turned to Sofia.

"Are all the vampires tied down now?"

"Yes, it looks like it."

"Then instruct the others to return to their subs. They must follow this submarine closely. And you should return to our submarine and follow us there too."

Sofia nodded and rushed off. Once I was sure that everyone who was due to leave this vessel had left—leaving me with Vivienne, Xavier, and a few others to help make sure the sedated vampires remained in their docile state—I ordered the blonde vampire to start our journey.

Chapter 36: Rose

I stared at the vampire, barely daring to believe his words.

Home.

He's taking me home.

"B-but," I stammered, "what about Stellan? Won't he tell the witch everything as soon as he wakes up?"

Caleb shook his head.

"He shouldn't wake up for some time after the blow I dealt him. But it doesn't matter even if he does. I've locked him up in one of the storage rooms in the lower deck of this submarine. He'll be weak after he wakes up and won't have the strength to smash the reinforced door down."

"What will you say when the witch asks what happened to

me?"

"That's not your concern."

"But what will happen when Stellan wakes up?"

Caleb looked at me darkly. "I'll deal with him when the time comes. But you'll be gone by then."

I breathed out and sat back in my chair. Escape had been on my mind for so long, now that it was finally happening, I could barely believe it.

"I can't tell you when or how it will happen, but you have my word: I will be waiting and watching for that time."

Caleb had been waiting. All that time, he'd been waiting for the opportunity to help me escape. I guessed that he hadn't had much time to plan any of this. He'd likely figured out this whole scheme on the spot.

Strapping himself into the control seat, Caleb fiddled with buttons and we began speeding away from the island.

"Do you even know where The Shade is?" I asked.

"No."

"Then how are we going to get there? I have no idea how to navigate there."

"Your parents aren't in The Shade."

"What?"

"They're in Stellan's island. They're storming the place, looking for you."

I gasped.

"Have they found Ben? And what about Kristal and Jake? How on earth did they find it?"

"I don't know all the details. But yes, they have Ben now. I don't know about the other two humans. Stellan struck a deal with your parents. You and your brother, in exchange for your immune."

I stared at him, my mouth agape.

"Our immune? Why would—"

"I don't know why," Caleb replied. "Annora doesn't tell me everything."

"So, Stellan was going to hand me over to my parents?"

"No. They thought they could trick your parents to hand over the immune, while in return giving them your brother only. Stellan escaped from your parents and came to take you away somewhere else in case The Shade's vampires managed to storm my island."

"Why would the witch want to keep me?"

Caleb shrugged.

"An extra bargaining chip against The Shade. Perhaps there are other things that you have over there that would be useful to us."

"Did they hand over Anna? Our immune?"

"I don't know."

I sat back in my chair, breathing deeply as I tried to absorb all this information. My heart was pounding at the thought of Anna's life being in danger. She was loved dearly by all of us. My parents had told us how she had saved Ben when he was just a baby. If it hadn't been for her, I likely would not have had a brother. What made things more worrying was that she was heavily pregnant. I prayed that my parents had managed to keep her safe. I couldn't imagine them ever handing her over.

"How long will it take to get there?" I asked anxiously.

"Perhaps another half an hour. It's not far."

My stomach was in knots for the rest of the journey. Finally, Caleb brought us to the surface. He moored up in some sort of port and then stood up. Rummaging around in the compartment above me, he pulled out a long dark cloak and a pair of sunglasses. I gasped when he drew out a dagger from his belt and cut a large gash in his palm. He dripped his blood all over the cloak, rubbing it into the fabric. His palm healed quickly, so he had to cut himself several times before enough blood had soaked into the fabric.

"Now, put these on," he said, handing me the cloak and shades. "My blood will help to mask the smell of your own. And keep that hood pulled down over your face."

I did as instructed and followed him toward the hatch entrance.

"Wait here," he whispered down at me.

I watched from below as he raised his head out of the

hatch and looked around.

He reached down for me. His hand enveloped mine in a strong grip as he pulled me up. He lifted me out of the hatch and placed me on the ground. I shivered. This place was as cold as Caleb's island. It seemed that the witch had cast the same spell over both.

Getting down himself, he stood in front of me, his muscular frame concealing me from view against the submarine. He turned around and looked down at me.

"You're going to need to stick close to me until we find your parents. Understood? Follow me like you're my shadow."

Holding my arm tightly, he held me close against him as we moved forward. I couldn't see much, given the dark shades and hood pulled right over my eyes, and I dared not lift either after Caleb's stern instruction. I could only see what was on the ground a few feet ahead of me.

We had barely been walking five minutes when he hissed, "Duck down!"

He pushed me down behind a bush. He knelt beside me. I held my breath as I tried to listen to what was going on. He parted the shrubbery and peered through it.

"They're leaving," he whispered.

"Huh?"

He parted the bush a little more and I raised the hood and

sunglasses. We were still near the port—we had been walking along the outskirts of the dark island—and I looked just in time to see a submarine submerging. Even though I only caught the top of the submarine, I knew it was one of The Shade's subs from its distinctive design.

Before I could say another word, he lifted me up and raced back to our submarine. Flinging open the hatch, he lowered me inside and shut it after him. He raced back to the control room and lurched the vessel forward before I even had a chance to reach my seat.

"We can't lose them," he said. "Or we'll have no way of getting you back to The Shade."

I gripped my seat as we surged forward. As I looked through the front screen at the dark waters we were traveling through, I couldn't see anything, but from the way Caleb was navigating the vessel, it was clear that he was following something.

But something didn't seem right. Home was the last place my parents would have been traveling to if they had been unable to find me on Stellan's island. They had found Ben, but I couldn't imagine them returning home without me.

"Do you think they're definitely heading back to The Shade?" I asked.

"It looks like it. At least, they're not headed toward my island."

I wondered if perhaps they had to return some injured vampires back to the island before coming back to search for me.

I settled more comfortably in my chair and looked up at Caleb's face. His eyes were fixed forward. As the hours passed by in silence, his concentration didn't break. I assumed that we definitely were headed toward The Shade since Caleb hadn't said anything to indicate the contrary.

This is it now.

I'm going home.

I'd thought I would be feeling joy and relief.

Instead, watching Caleb speed the vessel forward, I felt strangely numb.

Chapter 37: Rose

A few hours later, the vessel ground to a halt.

I glanced up at Caleb. He stood up and walked out the door. He headed toward the hatch and pushed it open, then lowered himself back down, making way for me to climb up.

Shivers ran down my spine as I looked up at the open hatch.

Just a few steps up toward goodbye forever.

He raised his eyes to me and, reaching for my hand, planted a chaste kiss over it.

"Goodbye, princess," he said softly.

He motioned to let go of my hand, but I gripped on tight. I began shaking my head.

"No. Not yet. Come with me," I said, tugging at him to climb up through the hatch with me.

"No. This is where I leave you."

"Caleb, you're coming with me whether you like it or not." I began climbing the ladder to the open hatch, gripping his arm and pulling him with me with all the force I could manage.

Sighing, he caught hold of a pipe sticking out of the wall and pulled himself back.

"Don't."

"Look, it's just for a short while. I promise. Please?"

He frowned at me. "For what?"

"I want you to meet my parents. Th-they'll want to thank you for everything you've done."

He looked even more reluctant at the mention of my parents. But after several more minutes of my begging, he eventually gave in to my request and followed me out of the hatch.

Looking around the port, I saw the large submarine moored in the harbor. I caught his cold hand, and, entwining my fingers with his, walked toward the entrance of the woods.

I watched his face as he took in the surroundings of our warm island. His expression was a mixture of fascination and apprehension.

"Mom?" I began to shout. "Dad?"

If they were on this half of the island they would hear me easily. One of the many benefits of having vampires for parents.

No reply.

But then a few moments later, my grandfather came into view, rushing along the forest path toward us.

"Grandpa!" I yelled, running toward him.

His face broke out into a huge smile and tears of relief filled his eyes as he swept me up in his arms. "Rose! Oh, Rose! I don't remember the last time I slept. We've all been sick with worry." He showered my cheeks with kisses and hugged me tight before finally putting me down. "How did you get here?"

"This is Caleb," I said, smiling and tugging at Caleb's sleeve. "He's the only reason I'm here. Caleb, this is my grandfather, Aiden."

My grandfather stood up straight, his eyes settling on Caleb for the first time. He reached out for Caleb's hand and shook it. Then he pulled Caleb against his chest for an embrace.

"I don't know anything about you, boy. But I'm forever in your debt for returning my granddaughter to me."

Caleb nodded, and gave him a small smile.

"Where's Ben?" I asked.

My grandfather's smile faded and worry creased his forehead.

"We found him unconscious in one of Stellan's submarines. He still hasn't come to, but we're hoping he'll be okay. Corrine's treating him now in the Sanctuary."

"What about Mom and Dad?"

"They're still looking for you. As soon as we realized you weren't with Stellan, your father managed to coerce one of the vampires there to reveal the location of his island. Vivienne, Xavier and a large group of other vampires are still with them storming the place and searching for you. I had to return early with Corrine and a few other witches in one of the submarines to care for your brother."

"And Anna?"

"She's here too. She's been here all along. Your parents never planned to hand her over. They pretended to have her just so they could ambush their submarines… but that's a long story. Now I must call your mom."

He reached into his pocket and, pulling out a phone, dialed my parents.

"Sofia? Darling, I've got her. Rose. She's here. Your daughter is back here in The Shade. No, I'm not joking. What kind of a joke would that be? You want to talk to her? Yes, of course. Hold on a second."

He passed the phone to me.

"Mom?"

"Oh, God. Rose!" My mom began gasping. I heard her pull away from the phone and yell, "Derek! Rose is back home! We can leave now! Yes, she's back!" She returned to speak to me. "Sweetheart, are you all right? Are you injured? How did you get back?"

"Mom, yes, it's me. I'm fine. A handsome knight in shining armor rescued me," I said, winking at Caleb. He smirked and rolled his eyes. I could have sworn I saw a slight blush in his pale cheeks.

"We're coming home right now, honey. We'll be back as fast as we can, in a few hours. Just stay where you are. Don't go anywhere."

"Don't worry, Mom," I said, half laughing. "I don't plan on going anywhere."

No sooner had I put the phone down than someone shouted out my name.

I turned around to see Griffin racing toward us. His face was pale, and he had dark circles under his eyes. He looked as though he hadn't slept properly for days.

"Rose?" he gasped as he reached me.

I wrapped my arms around him and I felt him cling to me, breathing heavily against my neck.

"You have no idea how much we've all been worrying about you."

"Griff, I can't tell you how sorry I am. What we did was incredibly stupid. I—"

"How the hell did you escape?" he asked, looking down at my face.

I took a step away from him and reached for Caleb's arm, pulling him closer to me.

"This is Caleb. He helped me escape. Caleb, this is my friend Griffin."

I watched as Griffin stared at Caleb as though he didn't know what to make of him. His expression was a mixture of surprise and distrust.

"Well, thank you," he finally said, patting Caleb on the shoulder. "I'm not sure what I'd do without this girl."

I stared at Griffin, surprised by the strength of emotion in his voice as he spoke those last words. We were close friends, but I supposed that I had never quite realized just how much I meant to him.

Griffin turned back to face me.

"Are you all right?"

"Yes, I'm not harmed. I just have a few scratches." I squeezed his hand, hoping to reassure him. "But I really need to see my brother now."

Chapter 38: Caleb

Rose insisted that I stay on the island until her parents returned. Although I felt uncomfortable, something made me give in to her requests. Perhaps it was just because she was so stubborn.

After greeting Aiden and her friend, we headed to see Rose's brother in a beautiful white stone building they called the Sanctuary. Walking through the hallways, we stopped outside a circular bedroom where Ben lay in the center of a bed. His eyes were open by the time we arrived.

"Ben!" Rose yelled and ran over to him, planting a kiss on his forehead and embracing him.

"Rose," he whispered, coughing and rubbing his throat.

Compared to Rose, he certainly looked worse for wear. He had shadows beneath his eyes, his skin had a yellowish tinge to it and he looked much thinner compared to when I last saw him. I dreaded to think what Stellan had put him through.

I looked at the brown-haired witch who was attending Ben along with several other witches. Her face lit up as soon as she saw Rose enter and she wrapped her in a tight hug.

"How did you get here?" Ben asked.

Rose ran over to me and dragged me to his bed. "Caleb." The princess beamed up at me. "He saved me."

Ben looked up at me and smiled, nodding. "I remember you," he wheezed. "Thanks man, for saving her... and for trying to save me."

He reached up a hand and I shook it.

It made me uncomfortable how she was touting me as some kind of hero. Still, she was getting pleasure out of it, so I didn't say anything to her.

Rose stayed beside Ben for a while longer, but it was clear that he wasn't in much of a state to talk. The witches suggested we leave and allow him to sleep to speed up his recovery.

We left the Sanctuary with Aiden, emerging into the beautiful moonlit courtyard outside.

"Grandpa," Rose said, "I'm going to show Caleb around

the island for a bit, all right? I'll check back at the port in a couple of hours or so to see if Mom and Dad have returned."

"Okay, darling." Aiden gave his granddaughter another hug before we parted ways.

Once we were left alone, she looked up at me. Her beautiful face broke out into a smile. "So," she said, wrapping an arm around my waist and squeezing me against her playfully, "what do you think of The Shade so far?"

"It's quite impressive," I replied, looking back at the witch's temple.

"You've barely seen anything yet." She had a twinkle in her eye. "I want to take you to The Residences now, but it's a fair walk. Could you carry me? I'll tell you how to get there."

I bent down as she wrapped her arms around my shoulders, her legs around my waist.

I began to speed through the forest, following her directions.

"Okay, stop here," she said, as we approached a particularly tall redwood tree. I put her down and she pointed upward. I couldn't help but inhale at the sight above me. Magnificent penthouses sprawled out among the treetops. They looked more stunning than rumor had made them out to be.

We entered the elevator and rose to the top. Crossing the

veranda, she pushed the front door open and led me inside. She pulled me past a luxurious sitting room and along a number of glass-covered walkways until we reached a spacious oval bedroom.

"This," she said proudly, "is my room." She pushed the door wide open and gestured that I step inside.

I looked around the room from the outside, hesitating to step in. Somehow, it felt strange to be stepping into her private space.

Growing impatient, she tugged on my shirt and pulled me inside.

She walked to a corner of the room and pointed to a large stack of CDs.

"As you can see, they're mostly classical," she said, grinning. "Or at least that's my excuse for not being able to dance to club music... Now let me show you the Sun Room."

She led me back along one of the glass-covered walkways and we stopped outside another room. She pushed the door open to reveal a room lit so brightly with LEDs, it gave the illusion of sunshine. The walls were covered with a mural of a sandy beach.

"This room has some history for sure," she said. "My dad destroyed it once. Ripped it to shreds with his bare hands. He used to have a real tough time controlling his temper.

Then my mom decided to recreate it."

Next, she led me into the music room. Calling it a room was rather an understatement. It was more like a small hall. Wind and string instruments lined the walls and at its center was a large grand piano.

I walked around the circumference of the room slowly, taking a closer look at all of the instruments. *Only the best for the Novaks.*

Rose took a seat at the piano. I walked over to her as she began to play. But as I approached, she stopped. She moved up along the seat, requesting that I sit next to her. I acquiesced.

"Now you're a prisoner of *my* castle"—she grinned—"I'd like you to play for *me*, Mr. Caleb Achilles."

I smiled down at her and bowed my head. "Very well, your highness."

I sat down beside her and stretched out my fingers over the keys. Closing my eyes, I began to play. And as soon as I did, I felt glad that she'd made this request.

Losing myself to the music helped to ease the pain that had been eating away at me ever since the moment had arrived for Rose's escape.

When she rested her head against my shoulder, I still didn't open my eyes. I wanted to remain lost in that moment, with her warm body against me. I remained still, committing these few seconds into my memory. A memory I hoped I'd be able to draw on for the rest of time.

Her soft hand folded over my forearm.

"I wish you didn't have to go," she whispered, pain traced in her voice. Pain I recognized as constricting my own chest.

I opened my eyes to see her lovely face, the shadow of tears brimming in her emerald-green eyes.

I didn't know what to answer her.

My throat felt dry.

Without considering my actions, I reached out and brushed her warm, flushed cheek with my fingers.

Then a bang from the living room broke through the silence.

Quickly composing myself, I stood up in time for Mr and Mrs Novak to enter the room.

Chapter 39: Rose

"Rose!"

My parents drew me into a tight embrace, kissing every part of my cheeks and forehead they could reach.

"What happened?" my mom asked, pointing to the bandage on my cheek.

"Oh, it's really nothing. Just a scratch."

Once we had finished hugging, I took a step back and reached for Caleb's hand. "This is Caleb," I said. "I'm here because of him."

My dad looked Caleb over from head to foot, as though he was sizing him up. I wasn't sure if he approved of Caleb at first, given the serious expression on his face, but then he smiled, reached out a hand and shook his warmly.

"Caleb," he said. "Thank you."

My mom drew him in for a hug. "If there's ever anything we can do to repay you," she said, gripping his shoulders and looking him in the eye, "please don't hesitate to ask."

"Nothing will be required," Caleb said, taking a step back.

"Rose!"

Vivienne and Xavier came racing into the room, followed by a group of other vampires. My aunt and uncle took it in turns to hug me. Then I faced the others. Everyone in the room—including my parents—looked utterly disheveled, their clothes bloody and torn, scars of recently healed wounds covering their body.

As I looked around the room at them, a crushing sense of guilt welled in the pit of my stomach.

Ben and I caused them all so much trouble.

"You," Zinnia said, pointing an accusing finger at me, "have caused me more aggro in the last twenty-four hours than Gavin has managed in the past year." Then she nuzzled me on the head. "I'm glad you're safe, kid."

Someone tugged on my hair. I turned around to see Ashley glaring at me.

"So, how was Scotland?"

I couldn't help but laugh at the sarcastic expression on her grimy face.

"Yeah, princess. How was Scotland?" Claudia had entered the room, her clothes looking particularly battle-worn, her thick blonde hair a matted mess. "Next time the two of you decide to go gallivanting about, a little warning would be appreciated."

"I'm so sorry, guys," I muttered.

"I should hope so," Eli said, crossing his arms over his chest and looking down at me sternly. "You both are exceedingly lucky to be alive. We honestly thought that we'd lost you."

My parents broke through the crowd and approached me. My father put his hand on my shoulder. His fierce eyes always melted me.

"You're going to get an earful from us too later, don't you worry," he said. "But for now, we're going to check on your brother."

He bent down and placed a kiss on my head. Then they left and the others trickled out too after them, leaving Caleb and I standing alone in the music room once again. He had moved over to a corner as soon as the crowd of vampires had entered.

One look at his ashen face, and I knew what he was about to say.

Chapter 40: Rose

"I need to leave now."

I realized that inviting him onto the island had been nothing more than an excuse to delay this moment.

Gulping back the lump in my throat, I nodded. I looped my arm through his and we walked out of the music room, through the corridors and out of the penthouse. Neither of us spoke a word as we took the elevator down to the ground and made our way back along the forest path toward the Port.

Throughout The Shade's history, the Port always had been a place of goodbyes. But I had never hated the place as much as I did now.

I walked with him until he stopped at the edge of the jetty.

His breathing mirrored my own as he looked down into my eyes one last time. Heavy. Constricted.

"I'd rather not drag this out any longer," he said, his voice husky as he detached my arm from his.

I nodded, biting my lip to prevent it from trembling.

"Goodbye," he said.

"Goodbye."

He turned and motioned to climb back through the hatch.

"Caleb," I stammered just before he lifted himself off the ground.

He turned to look back down at me, frowning.

"What?"

"If there's ever a way you can free yourself from that island… Please, come back here."

He froze at my words, his chocolate-brown eyes locked on mine. Then something sparked in them that I had never witnessed in such intensity. Passion. Desire. Fire. Before I could even realize what was happening, he'd leapt back down and wrapped an arm around my waist, pulling me close against him. Gripping the base of my neck with his other hand, he forced his lips against mine.

The strength of his hunger for me overpowered my ability

to return it in kind. I closed my eyes and reached my hands into his hair, gripping it and pulling myself closer against his body. Breathing in his scent, I relished every second that his tongue brushed against mine.

And then just as abruptly, it was over.

Still breathing heavily, he pulled away.

"I don't belong in your world, Rose."

He lifted himself up against the vessel and a few seconds later, he was gone.

When the hatch clicked shut, I could no longer hold back the tears. The ache in my chest consumed me.

Damn this cruel port and its tradition of first-and-last kisses.

As the submarine disappeared beneath the waves, it felt like a piece of me was drowning with it.

Chapter 41: Aiden

My life and the lives of most other vampires on this island had been utterly taken over by the disappearance of the twins. We'd used every hour of the day worrying about them and trying to locate them.

Although Ben appeared shaken by whatever he had gone through in Stellan's island—far more shaken than Rose—the twins were back.

Life can finally return to normalcy.

The first thing I did was seek out Adelle. She'd been worried sick just like the rest of us, but she hadn't come with us on any of our excursions because she—along with Abby and a few other witches—had to keep up their duties looking after the children on the island.

I suspected that at this time of day she might still be in her office in the school. I raced through the corridors and knocked on the door, relieved to see that my guess had been correct.

She stood up, her eyes widening as soon as she saw me.

"What's going on?" she asked, hurrying over to me.

"They're back," I panted. "Both twins are safe."

She clapped a palm over her forehead and breathed out.

"Oh, thank heavens. It feels like this whole island has been holding its breath for their return."

"Ben's extremely shaken by whatever happened to him," I continued. "He has refused to talk about details with anyone yet. But at least physically, he's recovering under Corrine's expert care."

"And Rose?"

"She seems to be fine. A few scratches, but nothing to speak of."

"I can't tell you how relieved I am," Adelle said, leaning against a desk and brushing hair away from her face with the back of her sleeve.

Mirroring her body language, I leaned against the chalkboard.

"Things can finally return to normal," I said.

"You look exhausted," she commented, eyeing me.

I nodded. "I think I'm going to go and get some rest. I just wanted to make sure you'd heard the news first."

"Thank you." She nodded, smiling. "Much appreciated."

"And... uh, there also was one other thing I wanted to say."

I stood up straight, dipping my hands into my pockets as I took a few steps closer to her, casually closing the distance between us.

"And what's that?" she asked, her eyebrows arched.

"Adelle, I—"

The door crashed open and Sofia sped in, her face alight with panic, sweat dripping from her brow.

"Have you seen Anna?" she panted.

"No," I said, walking up to my daughter and gripping her shoulders. "What's wrong, darling?"

"Kyle said she's disappeared."

Adelle and I both stared at Sofia, dumbstruck.

Chapter 42: Sofia

I stood staring across our kitchen table at Derek.

"A setup," I murmured.

"What else could this be?" He glared back at me. "As soon as they realized we'd shown up without Anna, those vampires had Caleb concoct an excuse to enter this island on the strength that he was returning Rose. And while he was here, he swiped Anna."

His words sent my head into a tailspin. Every inch of the island had been searched. Anna had well and truly disappeared. Kyle was distraught, although he was trying to put on a brave face for Ariana and Jason.

"I can't believe we could have been so stupid and gullible

as to trust that vampire," Derek seethed, throwing his hands in the air.

"Derek," I gasped, tears burning my eyes. "Anna's pregnant. She's eight months pregnant, goddamn it!"

I picked up a vase from the table and hurled it against the floor, shattering it into a thousand pieces.

I sank to my knees, fighting back the tears. I never had been one to express my feelings with violence, but this was about Anna.

Whoever is responsible for Anna's disappearance—be it Caleb or someone else—has just called upon a very different side of me than anyone is used to witnessing.

Chapter 43: Caleb

I swore as soon as the hatch slammed shut above me.

The taste of Rose was still alive on my tongue, her scent still haunting my senses.

What the hell was I thinking?

I stormed through the passageway and sat down in the control room, lowering the submarine as quickly as I could. Getting away as quickly as I could. *Away from her.*

As the dark waters flooded past us, I ramped up the speed.

"Hello, Caleb."

I whirled around to see Stellan standing a few inches away from me, a syringe between his fingers.

He stabbed it into my neck before I could react.

"Staying away for so many hours allowing me time to recover could have been excusable, but using one of my submarines to hold me captive in? You sure are a fool," he hissed in my ear as I sank to the floor. "I always keep keys on me." He lifted up a small chain of keys from a hidden pouch within his shirt and dangled them in front of me. He gripped me roughly and dragged my limp body out of the control room, down the steps toward the lower deck.

He stopped in front of the storage chamber. Before opening the door, he leaned down over me. His eyes glinting, he withdrew another syringe from his pocket and stabbed it into my neck. Blackness was clouding my vision fast now.

"Hm," he muttered loud enough for me to hear. "This dosage should be enough to keep you unconscious for just over seven days. Now I just need to decide where to dump you for all that time…"

He swung the door of the chamber open. I caught a glimpse of a young pregnant woman lying still in a corner before he flung me down against the hard floor and locked the door, plunging the room into darkness.

Ready for the next part of Derek and Sofia's story?

Please visit: www.bellaforrest.net for more information.

Also, if you visit: www.forrestbooks.com and enter your email address, you'll automatically get notified as soon as I have a new book release. (I will rarely send you emails—only to let you know when my next book is out.)

Thank you for reading,

Bella

P.S. Also, don't forget to come say hello on Facebook. I'd love to meet you personally:

www.facebook.com/AShadeOfVampire

Made in the USA
Middletown, DE
29 August 2016